W9-BEF-976

Danger
in the Desert

T. S. Fields

rising moon

www.northlandpub.com

www.northlandpub.com

The cover illustration was rendered in watercolor.
The display type was set in Crackhouse.
The text type was set in Berkeley.
Composed and manufactured in the United States of America

FIRST IMPRESSION, February 1997

01   02   03   04   05   10   9   8   7   6

ISBN 0-87358-664-6 (sc)

Library of Congress Cataloging-in-Publicaton Data
Fields, Terri
Danger in the desert / T. S. Fields.
p. cm.
Summary: Two brothers attempt to survive in the desert outside Scottsdale,
Arizona, after they are abandoned there following a carjacking.
ISBN 0-87358-664-6 (sc). — ISBN 0-87358-666-2 (hc)
[1. Kidnapping—Fiction. 2. Survival—Fiction. 3. Brothers—Fiction.
4. Deserts—Fiction.] I. Title.
PZ7.F47918Dan 1997
[Fic]—dc21   96-48667

To Rick and Jeff—two truly terrific guys.

Thanks to Doug Carty, manager of Arizona Reptile Center,
and Deputy James Langston of the Maricopa County Sheriff's Office
for their expertise.

All right, I admit that I shouldn't have brought the hose into the house and turned it on Robbie in the living room. But I wouldn't have done it if he hadn't "accidentally on purpose" thrown away the new Boy Scout badges that I'd worked so hard to earn. I knew I was in big trouble when Mom walked into the house while I still had the hose in my hand. At first, she just glared at us. Then she started to yell. "That's it! That's the final straw! For heaven's sakes, the two of you are not babies! You're nine and eleven." Then she turned just to me. "Scott, you are the oldest. I expect you to help your brother, not fight with him!"

"But he won't—," I started to explain before Mom cut me off.

"Yesterday, I came home from the grocery store to find Robbie had thrown your basketball shoe at the dresser mirror and broke it; today, you have the hose in the living room squirting Robbie. I don't know why the two of you cannot get along, but I will not have you destroying

1

this house." She threw us two big towels. "Clean this up. Then come with me. I will not leave you home alone anymore!"

That's why on a summer day, during my favorite shows on TV, we were trudging after our mother in the shopping mall. I never knew there were so many women's dress shops in one place or that it could be so boring to go into all of them. Waiting for Mom, I decided this mess was really Robbie's fault. If only he looked up to me the way little brothers should, we wouldn't always fight. Like why couldn't he ever appreciate any of the stuff I'd done in Boy Scouts? And I was sure that other little brothers didn't wear their All-Star baseball hats everywhere they went, just to remind their older brothers that they hadn't even made the All-Star team. But Robbie never took his red cap off his head except to sleep.

Finally, after my mom had even made us help her pick out a nightgown for Aunt Susan, she said she was ready to leave the mall. It had been three very long hours. We had almost gotten to the exit when Mom called, "Oh, look," and she pointed to a bright yellow sign with big red letters that read, "Get a Gulper of Root Beer. All Profits Go to The Literacy Foundation!"

Mom thought root beer sounded good, and as a teacher, she thought that supporting literacy efforts sounded even better. When the seller told her that sales had been rather slow, she bought four of the 44-ounce root beers in the fancy yellow containers even though there were only three of us. She said we could always drink an extra. The man selling the root beer looked so pleased, and as he snapped lids on the containers, he said hopefully, "You wouldn't like to buy five, would you?" Mom laughed and said four would be just fine.

We walked out of the air-conditioned Scottsdale Mall into the hundred-and-ten-degree heat. "It's a good thing we have these Gulpers. I'm already thirsty," Robbie said, his hazel eyes squinting into the sunlight.

"It sure is hot today," Mom said, trying to unlock the door of the station wagon without burning her fingers. "I don't know if I'll ever get used to these Arizona summers."

The summer after my dad died, we moved from Colorado to Phoenix. I was only seven then, but I remembered the move. I didn't want to leave our house. I begged Mom not to make us move, but she said we had to do it because this was where she'd gotten a job. She told me how I'd have to be a real grown-up, and I told her I didn't want to be grown-up if it meant I had to move to some dumb place I didn't want to go. But now, Phoenix seemed like home. I wasn't quite sure when that happened or why. I was just starting to think about that when, suddenly, I felt a jab in my back. "Hey, Mom's already in the car. And I called shotgun. I get the front seat!"

Mom leaned over, opened the passenger door, and fixed us with a look. "No fighting! Both of you can get in the backseat!"

The car was like an oven and we had finally just

begun to cool off around Bell Road when Mom decided we had better stop for gas. When she pulled in by the pump, we noticed a big sign that said, in bold black letters, "Prepay in the Mini-Mart before getting gas!" Unfortunately, the store looked crowded, so Mom left the motor running to keep the air conditioning working while she went in to pay.

"Hey," Robbie said, taking something out of the door handle well on his side of the car. "What's this?"

"What's what?" I said.

He dangled a small gold shape that looked like an upside-down smile in front of me. "My Scout Second-Class Badge. You give that to me right now! I've been looking everywhere for it. You probably took it and stuck it there so I wouldn't find it."

"Oops," said Robbie, grinning. He threw the badge under the front seat. "I guess I dropped it."

That did it. I pushed him onto the floor of the car and pounced on top of him. He may have been the better athlete. He may have been pretty strong for a kid his age, but he wasn't big enough or strong enough to move with my full weight wedged on top of him.

"I can't breathe," came Robbie's muffled voice.

"Tough," I hissed. "Find my badge and maybe I'll let

you up again." I heard the car door open, and Mom get in. I had the feeling we were about to be in big trouble for fighting again. Then I got a great idea. If I could sit up fast enough, Mom might not even realize that anything had happened. In fact, if I could get my seat belt on and let her notice that Robbie wasn't wearing his, he'd get in trouble, and I wouldn't. It was a great plan. Mom was nuts about safety. "Mom . . ." I started to say as I latched my seat belt. Then I looked at the figure in the front seat. It wasn't my mother; in fact, it wasn't even a woman! The car sped from the gas station and headed down a side street. I tried to speak, but nothing came out. Then finally, I yelped in surprise, "Hey! Who are you, and how come you're driving our car?"

I saw a pair of piercing brown eyes glare into the rearview mirror, and then the car swerved over to the side of the road and stopped. At that moment Robbie triumphantly popped up from the backseat. "See, Scott, you can't keep me down, and if you want your dumb old badge which I didn't . . ."

Robbie stopped in mid-sentence. His face went white, and his mouth opened, but no sound came out because in the front seat, he saw a man, and in that man's hand was a gun, and that gun was pointed right at my face.

I s that real?" Robbie's voice squeaked. "Who are you?"

"Shut up," the man said. His voice was real flat, as if he didn't care about anything or anyone.

I forced myself to move my eyes from the gun long enough to look at the man who was holding it. He had lots of greasy black hair that seemed to spring out from his head and he had thick, black, bushy eyebrows. His brown eyes were only slits, and they jumped angrily from Robbie to me. When they glared at me, I quickly looked away. The man swore softly and said, mostly to himself, "Just when I wonder what else could go wrong, I jack a car with kids in it."

My voice sounded scratchy. "We, uh, we could just get out, sir, and then this car wouldn't have any kids in it."

The man ignored me and looked at Robbie commandingly. "You, with the baseball hat, get up here in front next to me."

Still staring at the gun, I took a deep breath. "He's just a little kid. Leave him alone, and I'll climb up front."

The man leaned his face close to mine. I could smell alcohol on his breath. "I told you both—shut up."

The man got out of the car and opened Mom's packages in the back. He grabbed the nightgown that we had bought for Aunt Susan, made me put my hands behind my back, and wound the nightgown into a rope to tie my hands. He took a dress my mom had bought and wound it into another rope to tie my feet. Then he shoved me against the backseat and fastened a seat belt around me. When the guy had finished with me, I couldn't move at all. As he tied me up, he never said a word to me, and that made him even scarier. I couldn't help but notice the ugly, big scar running all the way down his left arm.

Somehow, as he was tying me up, he had managed to keep the gun pointed at Robbie's head. Then he barked at him, "In the front, now, right next to me. Just move my packages by the door. Do it!" he barked. "And be real careful with my stuff."

I saw Robbie's legs shake as he began to climb over the seat. "I . . . I'm coming right away."

He strapped a seat belt around Robbie, took the other seat belt and looped it around Robbie's neck. "You move— your neck could snap, okay?" The man didn't wait for an answer. He pulled a metal chain from his jeans pocket and flipped open a brown case to look at a watch. "I've already wasted too much time." Then he jumped into the front seat himself, gunned the motor, and took off for the freeway.

The car sped north on Scottsdale Road heading away

from Phoenix toward the desert. As cars passed in the other lane, I thought about trying to yell for help. But I couldn't be sure that the other drivers would hear or even if they did, that they would do anything. Besides, the gun the kidnapper had pressed to Robbie's neck kept me from trying it.

"Kidnapper!" I said softly to myself. There was an awful thud in my stomach. Everything had happened so fast that I didn't have a chance to think about how bad the situation could be. It was hard to believe this was real. I mean, Robbie and I had played cops and robbers hundreds of times, and we'd always fight because I'd say that I'd killed him so he should be dead. Then he'd shout that I'd missed him. But this was so weird. A part of me kept almost waiting for the guy to say that this was a game too, but the dry feeling in my mouth and the knots cutting into my arms and legs reminded me of just how real it all was.

It always seemed so easy on TV. Tons of times, I'd watched people get kidnapped, and they'd all been saved before the final commercial. Of course, they were the stars, and they had to live for the next show. We certainly weren't TV stars; we were just two kids. We didn't have any super powers; we didn't have any secret weapons.

The car hit a pothole, and the kidnapper grunted. I held my breath as the car's bounce made the gun shove further into Robbie's neck. This was even worse than anything I'd dreamed in my worst nightmare.

It'll be okay, I told myself. *By now, Mom has called every police agency there is. Someone will recognize this car any minute, and then the police will save us.*

I said this to myself over and over again until I felt a little better. I looked up to see if I could see any helicopters flying overhead, but there didn't seem to be any yet. I wished I could talk to Robbie. All the times I'd told him I never wanted to speak to him again, and now, I would have given anything to talk this over with him, but we couldn't very well talk about how to get free with the kidnapper right there listening.

When I looked out the window again, I saw another station wagon pass us. It was the identical cream color, with a beige interior just like ours. I bit my lip as I thought about how many times we had accidentally walked to the wrong car in a parking lot because so many people in Phoenix had our same kind of car. How could the police ever know which one was ours unless they could get so close they could see our license plate?

The man swerved into the other lane, and his packages hit the passenger floor. I wondered what was in them. Maybe he had more guns. Maybe he had a bomb. I tried hard to keep from totally panicking. Poor Robbie. It must be even worse sitting right next to the guy with a gun at your neck. I thought about saying something to Robbie, but I was afraid it might make the guy use the gun, and besides, what could I say that would make things any better?

I wished my hands were free. Then maybe I could signal one of the passing cars without the kidnapper seeing. I had to lean forward a little to keep my back from jamming into my tied hands, and I was beginning to feel sharp pain from the tightness of the scarf and the position in which I had to sit. I tried to move my hands, but they were tied so tightly that I could not budge them. A creeping numbness and a funny tingling began to move up my arms.

"Stop!" I wanted to yell at the other cars on the road. "How can you just drive on having a normal day when my brother and me are being kidnapped!" But of course, I didn't really yell anything, and I couldn't move my hands to make signals. *Think!* I told myself. *There must be something I can do.*

I stared at the rearview mirror to see if the kidnapper was watching me, but he wasn't, so I turned my face toward the window and silently mouthed "Help us!" to a car that passed. It sped on. I tried with each passing car to catch someone's attention, but no one noticed until, at last, a boy about my age in a blue sedan started staring at us.

The boy watched me carefully. His car was in the lane next to us, and it stayed even with us. I could tell by the way he stared that he knew something was wrong. My heart pounded when I saw him poke his mother and say something. Carefully, I mouthed the words, "Help! Kidnapped!" even more slowly. The boy watched intently. This family was going to help us! I had to make sure they understood. "Help, we're being kidnapped!" I mouthed again silently. My lips hurt from making each word so clearly. "Call the police," I carefully mouthed.

Suddenly, the boy nodded, smiled at me, then put his hands in his ears, stuck out his tongue, and made a funny face. He waved as his family's blue sedan turned off onto Dynamite Road. He thought it was all just a game.

I felt tears sting my eyes. No one was going to pay any attention to us. My arms felt like needles were shooting through them. I wished I could get loose. I began to move around. "Don't do that," came a command from the front seat, and the kidnapper pressed the gun into Robbie's neck.

"Okay, I won't move again; I promise . . . really. You don't have to stick that—that thing into my brother's neck so hard," I pleaded.

"You shut up. I'll decide where I keep my gun," said the kidnapper's cold voice.

"Okay, I'm sorry," I gulped, afraid to say more. Some big brother I had turned out to be. No wonder Robbie never listened to me about anything. I was always telling him I was almost three years older and knew much more, but what had I done to help either one of us get out of this mess?

Just then, the kidnapper made a sharp turn off the pavement and onto a dirt path in the desert. He slowed way down, but the car still jounced and bumped along the disappearing road.

How can this nightmare just keep getting worse? I

wondered as all the signs of the city disappeared, replaced by only desert rock, cracked earth, and cactus. But it did. We were going farther and farther away from any possibility of help.

The kidnapper seemed to know where he was going, but I didn't understand how because everything around us looked the same. From Boy Scouts I knew that it was dangerous to be out in the summer afternoon desert without lots of water, and I knew we didn't have that. Part of me said it was crazy to even think about enough water when there was some psychopath with a gun in the front seat, but I did. The car banged over a rock. My brother was so silent. He hadn't moved a muscle. "Robbie, you doin' okay?" I said softly.

"Shut up!" The man growled.

"What—what are you going to do with us?" Robbie's voice was real scratchy.

I prayed that the kidnapper would say that he was going to let us go, but he said nothing at all. The silence in the car suggested lots of terrible possibilities. The man moved his hand on the steering wheel. I don't know how I missed seeing it earlier. Maybe my eyes were too scared, but right then my stomach was doing flip flops as I stared at the big red snake tattooed on his right hand, and the way he moved his hand on the wheel, it was almost as if the snake was driving.

Then, in the quiet of the desert, I heard a noise in the distance grow louder, and I saw a gold Jeep come roaring toward us. *Oh, please,* I prayed. *Let this be some kind of a desert ranger.* The Jeep stopped in front of us, and a man with stringy, long brown hair and a big earring in one ear swaggered toward us. He was bigger than the kidnapper, and he didn't look like help for us. As he pulled open the door to the station wagon, I saw that he, too, had a big black gun.

"Hey, Slam," our kidnapper called.

Slam complained, "It sure took you long enough to get here." Then he noticed us. "What the—!" he yelled.

"Long story. Bad luck," the kidnapper replied, getting out of the car.

"Yours or theirs?" Slam asked.

"Both, I guess." There was a flat, dead tone in the guy's voice that terrified me. The two men moved away from the car a little, but kept their guns on us as they talked. Although I could only hear little pieces of their conversation, I caught some words about offing a guy, stealing money, and needing a car, and I thought I heard something about heroin as they moved back toward us.

Slam cocked his gun. "You want to do one, or should I kill 'em both?" He asked the question like it was no big deal.

"Doesn't much matter to me who kills them," our kidnapper said. "Let's load this stuff into the Jeep first."

These guys were going to kill us, and we couldn't do a thing to stop them. Even if I could get loose and get Robbie out of the car, the desert was flat and wide open. Picking us off would be easy. Everything started to feel as if it were moving in slow motion. My mouth felt loaded with cotton, and my throat could barely swallow. I was paralyzed, and I was sure Robbie must be too.

Paying no attention to our frozen fear, the two men went to the back of the the Jeep with the packages the kidnapper had in our station wagon. Slam's voice rose, "You didn't bring the extra ammo? Of all the stupid—!"

"I told you. The car broke down. I could only carry the smack. Everything else stayed." The kidnapper's voice got soft and real scary. "Is that a problem?"

Slam spit on the ground, but he didn't argue. "Well then, we're not wasting what we got on them." He gestured his gun toward us.

Our kidnapper shrugged. "I don't care either way."

14

Slam started the Jeep; our kidnapper jumped in, and they roared off into the desert without a backward glance.

Almost like a robot who hadn't been programmed to move, I watched the cloud of dust that the Jeep made until it was just a speck in the distance. My throat felt as if it had a huge lump of something blocking it, but I choked out, "Robbie, you okay?"

"I think so, are you?" Robbie whispered back, still too frightened to turn around.

"They're gone!" My voice was starting to come back. I sobbed, "They're really gone. They're not going to kill us. We're free! Robbie, you hear me?"

"Free?" Robbie half-whispered. "Free!" he said loudly in joy. "We're not gonna die!"

"Robbie, can you get out of the front and untie me? He's got these things so tight, I don't have any feeling in my arms."

"Okay." Robbie moved almost as if in a trance. He undid the seat belt that had been slung around his neck, unfastened the one that had strapped him in, and opened his door. He got out of the car shaking his head and rubbing his eyes almost as if he had just awakened from some bad dream. Finally, he opened my car door and began to tug at my bindings. As I watched him work, I wondered how it could be that my ropes had been only clothes from a shopping trip an hour earlier. Somehow, it seemed as if that shopping trip must have been a whole lifetime ago.

"Sorry, I'm really trying. I can't get 'em loose. He tied

15

everything so tight," Robbie said, and I could see the sweat on his forehead. He tugged and pulled. "There! I got it!" he yelled.

Finally, I was free. My arms felt like two big, dead trees at my sides. I forced myself to shake my hands, and then I forced my hands to rub my arms and legs. Feeling began to return to them, and I groaned loudly. It felt the same as when I'd cracked my elbow on something, only this wasn't just my elbow; it was both of my arms and my legs. Little needles of pain shot up and down them. "Ohhhh," I moaned.

"Hey, you gonna be okay? What can I do?" Robbie shouted.

I forced myself to keep moving and stretching, and finally, the pain went away. Looking at my hands, I opened and closed my fists. Everything still worked! It was a miracle. I looked at Robbie and grinned. "I'm okay and we're alive and we're free. You can't keep the Ratliffe brothers down!"

The freckles on Robbie's nose stood out, and his face was real white. "Wow, that was the most . . . the most . . ." Robbie paused as if he didn't know words to describe exactly what it was. "That guy, he was really the worst . . . I mean when he had that gun in my neck . . ." He paused again. "Geez, am I ever glad he's gone. I hope I never see anyone like him again." Then he wrinkled up his nose. "Boy, wait until I tell Marc, and Josh, and Ricky. Ricky thinks he's so tough. He never had to face any kidnapper!"

All of a sudden, his eyes lit up. "Hey, you know what I think?" Without waiting for me to say anything, he blurted, "I bet we're gonna be on TV. I bet we're gonna be famous. I get dibs to be on TV first and tell all about what happened to us."

We were both wound up with the amazement of still being alive and being free. I jumped right in: "Nah, I'll get to be the one on TV. Your red hair will be too bright for the cameras. The TV people will all want to talk to me, but don't worry, I'll tell 'em your name."

It felt so good to be talking about normal stuff like TV and to be arguing with Robbie! He punched me lightly on the arm, whooped, and ran around the car. I knew just how he felt. Being alive at this moment was better than having no homework for a whole school year, better than hitting a home run with bases loaded. Robbie laughed and so did I. Robbie tossed his baseball hat into the air and whooped! "Wow, for a little while, I really did think those guys were gonna—"

"Yeah, I really thought—," I interrupted and then stopped myself. Robbie was still just a little kid. There was no point in scaring him with what I thought was going to happen. Besides, everything was okay now.

We grinned at each other and continued talking about the guy and his gun. Robbie was going a mile a minute, and after a few sentences, I knew he didn't even care if I listened; he just had to talk. It was fine with me. I was thinking my own thoughts. I had never even really considered what it might be like for me to die. It had just seemed like something that would happen someday when I was real old. Suddenly, I felt Robbie pulling on my shirt. "Hey, Scott, I said what do you think?"

"About what?"

"About getting out of here. It's really hot."

"Right," I said. "But before we just take off, maybe we better have some kind of plan."

"It'll be easy," Robbie said. "The kidnapper drove us into the desert; we'll just drive ourselves out. I saw a mountain to our right as we turned onto the desert road, so if we just turn the car around and keep the mountain to our left, we should be just fine." Robbie grinned a look that said, *See? Your nine-year-old brother is smarter than you thought.*

"Uh, jerk-brain, look around real good."

Robbie squinted into the distance. Rock and stone mountains seemed to go in every direction. Robbie's face grew beet red, and he didn't say anything else. Then I realized he wasn't red just because I'd shown him how silly his brilliant plan was. I was probably almost as red. We had been standing out there celebrating our luck in being alive for at least fifteen minutes, and the desert sun had been pounding into us. It had to be at least 120 or 130 degrees, and suddenly, the incredible happiness of being free was pricked by the fact that we were sort of lost in a burning hot place without any help except each other.

I stared at the ground, and then I had an idea. "How

about this. We'll follow the tracks the car made coming out into the desert until we get back out. I'll drive, and you can be my scout. I'll go real slowly, and you'll keep your eyes peeled on the road for tracks."

Sweat was pouring off Robbie's face, and without waiting for his reaction to my plan, I climbed into the driver's seat. Robbie took the passenger's front seat. "Uh-oh. I don't see any keys." That pit in my stomach was starting again. I wondered if they had taken the keys with them. No keys—no transportation. No transportation—well, I didn't want to even think about that. There was no way we could walk out of the desert, and it was much too hot just to hang around.

Suddenly, Robbie dug down behind the seat next to me, and he emerged smiling and holding Mom's keys. "I saw the guy throw them down here. Pretty good memory, huh?" It seemed to me that Robbie figured all the danger was over now that the kidnappers were gone, and that getting back home was some kind of a game. I wished I could think of it that way. "Hey, Scott," he asked, "have you ever driven a car before?"

"Uhh, sure." I lied with what I hoped seemed like confidence. There was no point to telling Robbie that I had only driven once, and that was when our uncle had let me steer. I hadn't been able to reach the pedals, so I wasn't sure whether it really counted as driving, but it would have to do. Actually, I could barely reach the pedals now and still see over the dash.

I put the key in the ignition just as I had watched

Mom do so many times, and then I put my foot on the gas. I turned the key, pressed on the pedal and hoped for the best. The motor raced; I felt a thrill, and we moved—absolutely nowhere.

Robbie looked disgusted. "I think you have to take the gearshifter thing off the P."

"Right," I said, "I knew that. I was just testing the power."

"Why?"

I didn't answer. Instead, sucking in a deep breath and hoping for the best, I moved the gearshift to D and we lurched forward. "Wow," I said almost to myself. "I'm driving. I'm really driving a car!" My heart was pounding so hard, I was almost sure even Robbie could hear it.

"Yeah," said Robbie. "But you're going the wrong direction."

I knew that. I really did. I just needed to get the feel of driving. This definitely wasn't like all the times Robbie and I had sat behind the wheel and pretended to drive. Real driving felt much different. It was scary, and I wished Robbie would just appreciate that we were moving without bumping into things. It was amazing to think that I was actually making this car head in a straight line.

Before I was at all ready to think about how to turn, Robbie stared at me and asked, "Well, are you sure you can turn this car around? If you can't, well, I could try." There was a note of impatience in his voice.

I took a deep breath. "'Course I'm sure I can turn the

car around. I just haven't driven Mom's car before, and I wanted to get used to it. Now quit worrying and just let your big brother take care of things."

It sounded good, but I knew that Robbie was right about getting turned around. I had to get us going in the right direction, or there was no point to going at all.

It was so hot that I could see wavy lines in the air. I just wished I had some idea how much you had to turn a wheel to make it move the car around. Robbie broke into my thoughts. "Okay, here's a great spot. It's flat, wide, and there's no cactus on either side. Now come on, turn the car around, so we can get going and put on the air. How can we ever get on TV and be famous if we keep going in the wrong direction?"

I began turning the wheel. The car bumped its way around the dirt path until finally the station wagon was facing the opposite way. My heart was pounding, and I had to wipe my sweaty hands on my shirt to keep them from sliding on the wheel, but we were headed home!

I turned the air conditioning on, and the car began to blow cool air. For the first time in hours, I began to feel almost normal. We would just follow this path until we got back to the freeway. I licked my lips. It had been a long time since I'd had anything to drink. I realized that the 44-ounce gulpers were still in the car somewhere, but I wasn't taking my hands off the wheel to get one, and I wasn't letting Robbie take his eyes off the path, either. I licked my lips again. The gulpers would have to wait.

The ride seemed to be getting rougher. The steering wheel was hard to hold onto as we bounced over each rock, but at least we were still moving. I just hoped we wouldn't hit anything sharp that would cause the tire to go flat. But I had to think positive. After all, we had made it all the way out here without a flat, why not all the way back?

I stared out the window, and it looked to me as if there were tracks on a dirt path over to the left. Yet Robbie was still insisting that we continue going right. I took my eyes off the road straight ahead, and I squinted to see where the tire tracks went toward the left.

"Yikes!" Robbie screamed.

Heart pounding, I rammed my foot on the brake. The car lurched, stopped, and died. "What's with you?" I started to say, and then I noticed that the front bumper of the car was almost touching the base of a large saguaro cactus.

I got out of the car to see if I'd hurt anything, and once I was in front of the car, I could see that the tracks off to the left were more like motorcycle tracks. Robbie saw me staring. "Hey, why do you always think I'm such a baby? I was following the right tracks."

"Sorry," I said.

"You're such a . . . " Robbie looked at me. I was fighting back tears, and I think he knew it. This was his chance to get me good, but I saw Robbie bite his lip. He just looked at me for a minute, then said, "Hey, it's okay.

You're doing a good job. Driving's probably tough."

I smiled. "Yeah, well you're a good navigator, and together, we're gonna get out of here." There was a kind of awkward silence. It was weird being nice to each other. It didn't happen very often. We climbed in the car, and I started it again. It was a little easier this time because at least I had already driven the car now, but when I went to back up, the car lurched, and I knew I hadn't quite figured out all the parts to this driving thing yet.

I started to hear scraping noises as we went forward, and as the car bumped and bounced along, I wondered how much we were tearing up the bottom of it. *Please,* I said silently, *don't let this car fall apart! Keep going.*

Robbie's voice started sounding tired as he continued calling, "More to the left here; move toward that path on the right." My hands hurt from holding onto the steering wheel so tightly. The game of driving had quit being fun after the first few minutes. There was just too much to worry about. Suddenly, it seemed that we were slowing down. I hoped that it was just that the road was rougher here, and I pushed the gas pedal harder, but instead of picking up speed, we slowly rolled to a stop.

"I said to go to the right," Robbie said and then warily asked, "Why are we stopping here?"

"I don't know." I took my aching hands away from the steering wheel and tried to think. Maybe I could raise the hood the way the mechanic did at the garage, but then what? What did I know about how the inside of an engine was supposed to work or what to do if it didn't?

Robbie got out of the car and looked at it. "The tires don't look busted. Maybe you should just try starting it again."

I put my hand toward the ignition, and as I did, my eye caught the instrument panel. Suddenly, I remembered  where we had been when this whole mess had started. "Robbie," I said, feeling about a million years old. "I know what's wrong." I tried to keep the fear out of my voice as I thought about being in the middle of nowhere with no help possible. "We just ran out of gas."

"Out of gas? No! Try again. We just can't be out of gas." I looked at Robbie, and under the red baseball cap, I saw him biting his lip and trying not to cry. I knew just how he felt. I didn't see how the car would start, but I could try it once more for Robbie's sake—and for my own.

Suddenly, Robbie reached across me and pulled the key from the ignition. "Hey, what are you doing?"

Almost frantically, he began rubbing the key against his T-shirt. "Something just got on the key, and if we clean if off, the car will start again. Don't you think?" Without waiting for answers, Robbie stuck the key back in the ignition.

I pressed my foot hard on the gas, and then I closed my eyes, took a deep breath, and turned the key. The motor chugged and died. I looked at the empty gas gauge and then I tried again and again. The car didn't move; it wasn't going to move. I put my arms across the steering wheel and buried my head in them. It all made sense, I thought to myself. Mom hadn't had a chance to get gas when the kidnapper had taken the car. He'd used up all that there was.

I felt all used up too. My head was too hot and too tired to think anymore. First, I'd tried so hard to think about how to keep Robbie and me from getting killed by the kidnappers; then I'd had to think about how to get out of the desert, and then how to drive a car. The hot sun poured into the car, and I just wanted to let myself go to sleep and not have to think anymore.

In the quiet, I could hear Robbie's muffled sobs. They forced me to pick up my head, and I reached out to touch his shoulder. "Hey, Rob, it's going to be okay."

"Okay?" Robbie didn't even try to stop crying. "How can you say it's going to be okay, when everything is so awful."

He was right. No wonder the kidnappers had been so willing to just leave us there. I didn't really see any way that anything was ever going to be okay again for us, but there was no point to admitting that and scaring Robbie even more. "Listen," I said, and I hoped my words would somehow come true, "it's going to be okay because we'll just spend the night here, and by tomorrow morning, a search party will find us."

"Spend the night here? No way!" Robbie's eyes got big.

He looked almost like something had snapped inside him. "I've had it! I'm not staying out here in the desert with the snakes and — and the other stuff that comes out at night, and you can't make me." His voice was coming in gulps. "And . . . and if this dumb car won't go, I'm—I'm just going to walk home!"

o!" I shouted. I knew from the little camping I'd done that we probably didn't have much chance out here, but if we started walking at night, we wouldn't have any chance at all.

Robbie opened the car door. "I'm going," he said stubbornly. "I'm just going to follow these tire tracks until I get back to the highway, and once I'm there, someone will give me a ride home."

"But we can't—"

Robbie cut me off. "Stop it. Stop telling me what I can't do. You just don't want me to have a good idea. You just don't want me to be the one who saved us." Robbie got out of the car and started to walk. I knew it would be pitch black, and he would be completely lost if I let him go, so I forced myself out of the car after him.

"Stop!" I called. "You can go after we talk, but at least listen!"

Robbie began to run from the car. "No, I'm not listening again!"

I watched him go a few feet and then took off after him. "Robbie, come on, cut it out," I called, but that only seemed to spur him on. It was so hot I could hardly breathe. "Robbie, stop. I won't come after you, I promise. Just stop where you are and listen to me, then if you want to go, you can." I was shouting at him.

He stopped running. "Okay," he shouted back, "but you stay right there. Tell me from where you are."

I took a deep breath and put my hands to my mouth to make my voice louder. Then I shouted, "Look at your watch. It's already six o'clock. How could we get out of here before it gets dark? We don't even have a flashlight. We'd be miles from the car, and all alone with whatever animals are out here. If you just wait until morning, we'll start walking out as soon as it gets light." My words tumbled out. "In the morning we'll have plenty of light, and it won't even be so hot yet. What do you think? You want to run into some animal when it's totally dark, and you can't even see what it is?"

For a second there was silence. At least Robbie hadn't turned to keep walking away. Then I saw him start back toward me. "You're right," Robbie mumbled, coming back to the car. "Guess I just didn't want to stay out here much. Sorry I yelled."

"Forget it." I licked my parched lips. "I'm real thirsty; let's find the gulpers."

We got back in the car, and Robbie dove under the seat and pulled all four gulpers out one by one. He tried to smile. "Good thing they came in these squeeze containers

with caps. They're almost still full. I just wish they were still cold."

"Yeah, good thing Mom wanted to support literacy! At least we have them." I was trying hard to remember what I had learned in Scouts about desert survival. I thought they had said that a person needed about a gallon of liquid a day to survive. Well, we had that now, but what if our rescue took longer?

"Boy this feels good," Robbie said, taking a drink.

I put the gulper to my mouth and took a swig of the root beer. It burned all the way down my throat, but even though it was warm and sticky-sweet, I'd never tasted anything better. I think I could have drunk the whole thing, but I made myself stop, and I pulled the other container from Robbie, telling him that we had to make it last.

Robbie looked at me, and he looked really weird. "Scott, if I ask you something, do you promise just to tell and not to laugh?"

I smiled. I don't know why. "Okay."

"Never mind."

"Come on, I promise," I said.

"Uh, well, uh . . ." Robbie moved around on the seat. "Uhhhh . . . I was just wondering if pee makes snakes come out in the desert?"

In spite of everything, I almost started to laugh, and then I realized that Robbie was serious. To tell the truth, I didn't remember any book saying anything about the subject, but I lied. "You know, there was something in my book. It said that you could pee in the desert . . ." Robbie was hanging on my every word intently, and at some other time, in some other place, this would have been a great trick to play on him, but in this awful place, I just wanted to make him feel better. "You could pee in the desert, and it didn't make any animals come at all."

Robbie looked at me. "You sure?"

"Positive!" I said.

Robbie smiled and got out of the car. "I'll be right back." He took off. It was weird. I'd had to go so bad while I'd been tied up in the car. I guess it was just fear. Anyway, the urge was gone now. I looked at the sun. As hot as it was, it was also clear that the sun had begun to set. I had camped out with the Scouts a couple of times, but Robbie had never slept outside. He had no idea how dark it could get, or what strange sounds the night made. I hoped Robbie wouldn't be too scared. Who was I kidding—I hoped I wouldn't be too scared! I wished with all my heart that some rescuers would magically appear and we could be back home.

My thoughts were interrupted by Robbie returning. "Boy, do I feel better. Now I'm hungry. I don't guess we've got much for dinner except the gulpers, huh?" Then his face lit up. "Hey, what about the Lifesavers Mom took away from us because we were fighting over who got the red ones?"

I took a package of them out of the glove compartment. "Good thing we fought, huh?"

I opened the roll, and Robbie and I stared at the Lifesavers, trying to figure out how to make them last. We decided, since they were our least favorite, to eat all the green and orange ones for dinner and put the rest away to have something good for the next morning. It was sort of funny. Candy and soda pop had always sounded like a great dinner, but now that we had them, they didn't make such a super meal. At least the candy and drink helped my throat, which no longer felt so dry that I couldn't swallow. I sucked the final piece of my last Lifesaver and leaned my head back against the seat. Robbie and I sat in silence. I looked at my watch. Ten minutes passed, and it felt like it must have been ten hours.

It was going to be a long night just sitting in that car. But then I thought about the kidnappers and remembered that we could have already been dead, so I told myself that it wasn't really so awful to sit there for one night. Still, it was so very quiet. I looked at Robbie, and saw him staring out the window. He had his arms on the door, and his face in his hands. He looked pretty down. "Want to play Twenty Questions?"

"Nah, maybe later," he said dejectedly.

Suddenly I got an idea. Why hadn't I thought of it before? This would be great! "Hey, watch this. A little music and a little cool air."

"What are you—," Robbie started to say. Then I turned on the motor, snapped on the radio, and flipped on the air conditioning.

"Wow! How'd you ever get that to work?" I thought Robbie looked impressed, and I was pretty impressed with myself, too. Music immediately filled the car, but

only warm air blew from the vents. "The music is great. It makes it seem, I don't know, not so empty, but geez, it's still sure hot in here. Why doesn't the air blow cool?"

I wasn't really sure. I reasoned that just because the car was out of gas didn't mean that the battery wouldn't work at least for a while, and if the battery worked, so did the radio. "I guess the battery makes the radio run and air come out, but you need gas for the air to get cool. At least it will get cooler after the sun goes down."

"Yeah." Robbie took off his hat for a minute. Sweat had made his hair stick to his head. "Let's change the station." Robbie punched a silver button on the radio. The music ended, and an announcer said, "Here are the evening's headlines. Today, in Phoenix, two young boys were kidnapped."

"Hey, that's us!" Robbie cried.

"Shhh, I want to hear."

The announcer's voice continued, "The boys' mother, Mrs. Janet Ratliffe, had just stopped for gas at the newly opened Mini-Mart on 32nd Street when a person or persons unknown stole her car. At this time, police have no suspects, nor do they know whether the purpose was to steal the car or the children."

"It was the car," Robbie broke in; "and we know all about the suspects."

"Shhh," I commanded.

"We have Mrs. Ratliffe with us on the air, and she wants to talk to her sons' abductors."

There was silence for a minute, and then Mom's voice filled the car. "Whoever you are who took my boys, please don't hurt them. Please let them go. They can't hurt you, and they mean the world to me." Mom sounded as if she was crying, and the announcer came back on. "If you have any information about these boys . . ."

"Mommy!" Robbie half-shouted the word. I snapped the radio off. I couldn't look at Robbie because I knew he was crying, and I didn't want to cry too. "Hey, it's okay, bud. Tomorrow, we'll be back with Mom, and everything will be okay. You heard the guy say that everyone was looking for us, didn't you?"

"Yeah, I just wish they could find us tonight instead of tomorrow."

I just hoped they could find us at all before it was too late. I looked out at the desert. It definitely was not a friendly place. It seemed to me that it was getting dark outside awfully fast. I tried to tell myself that it was just that the sun had been so hot, and now it was going down, but there was a strange kind of shadowy calmness outside.

Robbie must have felt it too, because I saw him squint toward the sky. "You think there are lots of animals out here at night?"

Actually, I did. In social studies last year, we'd learned

33

all about how it was too hot for most desert animals to be out in the day, so they came out at night, but I didn't know if I should tell Robbie that. Things were so weird. Ever since Robbie had been able to talk, I'd been waiting for him to treat me like an older brother who knew stuff. Now that he was finally doing it, I just wished there was someone older to take care of both of us out there. "Well, are there lots of animals out here?" Robbie asked again.

"Oh, some, but we'll be okay in the car. We'll have the windows up, and the doors locked. Good thing you didn't just take off walking."

"I didn't know it was going to get dark so fast. Wow, look at all those black clouds. Where'd they come from? Let's turn on the radio again and see if they're talking about us."

I ran one hand through my hair. "Robbie, the battery won't last forever. We have to wait to turn the radio on. If we keep turning it on now, we won't have it later."

Wind started blowing hard. "Please, just for a second?"

I leaned over and turned on the radio. What could a few seconds hurt. After having squinted against the sun all day, it was strange to see everything through the haze of darkness. Music blared from the radio, so I switched the station to see if there was any news on. An announcer's voice said, "Repeating. There is a flash-flood watch for the eastern Valley desert area. Do not travel in that area for the next two hours unless absolutely necessary. If you must be in that area, do not go near any desert washes."

The first few drops of rain hit the windshield, and I turned the radio off before Robbie heard any more. Robbie looked at me; I knew what he wanted to ask, but I wasn't going to offer the answer because I knew it would scare him even more than whatever he could be thinking.

Last year, for a grade in social studies, I did an extra credit project on flash floods in Arizona. I didn't remember all of it, but I did remember writing that lots of people died in flash floods because desert washes didn't look like river beds at all. They were a little lower than the area around them, but they were completely dry. Suddenly, heavy rain came, and in practically no time, the dry washes were raging rivers strong enough to uproot trees. People's cars even got stuck and sank, forcing the people to try to swim in a fast river or drown in their cars.

"Uhh, Robbie, I'm just going to go outside for a minute."

"How come? It's starting to rain. You're gonna get all wet, and then Mommy—," he stopped himself. I knew what he was going to say, that Mom would be mad. Boy, did I ever wish she was there to yell at us right then!

I was not going to tell Robbie that I was trying to check and see if we were in a desert wash, so I just said, "Yeah, think about it Rob. We've been so hot all day. Wouldn't the rain feel good?"

Robbie smiled. "Yeah, why didn't I think of that!" We opened our doors and got out of the car. To tell you the truth, the whole desert looked pretty flat as far as I could see. Of course, I'd never really seen a desert wash, so I wasn't sure what I was looking for, but I didn't think we were in one. Besides, I didn't think it was going to matter. The rain was barely coming down. The drops were so few and far between that the ground didn't even look wet. So much for enough rain to make a flood.

Then suddenly there was the most enormous blast in the sky. It sounded like a million guns all being shot at the same time. Robbie opened the door and dived back into the car. I stood frozen to the spot wondering what terrible thing was happening now. Maybe the kidnappers were nearby bombing stuff. Then I realized I had heard that sound before. It had just never been so fierce or loud in the city. Heart pounding, I opened the door to the car and looked at Robbie curled down on the seat. "It was just thunder," I said as if I'd known all along that the sound was no big deal.

"Oh, yeah, I knew that." Robbie sat up and tried to match my tone. "I just felt like getting in the car, that's all."

I looked at him, and smiled. He shrugged and grinned back. A wedge of lightning followed by another blast of thunder started quite a show. We rolled down the car windows, and we could feel the temperature drop. It felt so good. The desert darkness of heavy clouds made the lightning flashes something to watch. "Like our own laser show, huh, Robbie?" I said in awe.

"Yeah, definitely better than the show at the planetarium that Mom took us to."

"Okay sky," I commanded. "Let's have a bright chunk of lightning over there," and I pointed. Almost on cue, the lightning struck, and Robbie and I both laughed.

"Hey, let me try." Robbie shouted out the window. "All right thunder, listen up. I want the next blast when I say three. One, two—." A loud blast of thunder filled the air. When it subsided, Robbie shouted. "Hey, can't you follow directions? You were supposed to make noise after I counted to three, not two."

We both laughed. There was still almost no rain, and the wind had died down, too. We passed time by trying to conduct the lightning storm. Sometimes, it seemed as if the lightning and thunder were following our exact directions, and others, as if nature was paying no attention to our commands at all.

"Hey," Robbie said, after he seemed to get the lightning and thunder to follow him exactly. "Maybe I'll grow up to have a rock group, and I'll call it Lightning Power. My group'll be real famous, and we'll have laser stuff just like this behind us on stage. People will wait in line for tickets to our concerts for practically forever."

"I thought you wanted to be a pro baseball player," I said.

"Yeah, I do, but I could be a rock star in the off-season."

"Right. Maybe your group could do pregame shows."

"Nah. We'd be too famous for that. Besides, I'd be busy warming up my arm for the game."

"The only thing you warm on the bench is your rear!" I said.

"Ha, ha. Keep that up and I won't get you any free tickets to my games or my concerts!"

It felt pretty good just to be kidding around about stupid stuff. Then off in the distance we saw a huge piece of zig-zagging lightning that looked as if it almost hit the ground. "Wow," Robbie yelled. "Did you see that one?"

"Yeah," I answered. "I think that one was the biggest of all." There were more thunder and lightning blasts, but nothing like the huge one. Robbie and I joked as we continued to conduct our band, "Hey, turn up the volume again!" Then way off in the distance, I saw it.

"Geez," I half-whispered, pointing ahead and to the right. "That big lightning a few minutes ago; I think it started a fire." Robbie's eyes opened real wide as he looked in the direction I was pointing. Then another blast of thunder and bolt of lightning filled the sky, and we both jumped. I guess the dry desert must have been feeding the fire fast because as we stared at the orange speck, it kept growing into a brighter ball of orange and a line of smoke wound across the sky.

I drummed my fingers on the steering wheel and began to worry. If the thunder was louder than loud here, and the lightning was brighter and longer here than anywhere else, maybe fire traveled faster than it did anywhere else. I didn't think it could get to us. We were really far from it, but then I'd heard about how desert fires could burn hundreds of acres, and I had no idea how many acres we were from the fire. I tried to think, but I absolutely couldn't think of anything

39

we could do if the fire came our way. We couldn't outrun it, that was for sure. Our car wouldn't work and no one else was there, so I decided that all we could do was hope that the fire burned itself out long before it got to us. That wasn't very comforting. We had hours to sit there before morning. The desert was always really dry in the summer. Why should the fire burn out before it got to us?

"Wow, look at all that smoke in the sky!" Robbie exclaimed, and then I felt a glimmer of hope. Smoke . . . like smoke signals . . . like someone had to come and fight the fire. Didn't they? I tried to think if firemen only fought fires in the city, but I didn't think so. I knew they fought them in forests. I'd seen it on a TV movie, so they must fight them in the desert too. The smoke in the sky would bring firefighters, and then we'd be rescued. I turned to Robbie. "Boy, isn't that fire great?"

"Great?" he said questioningly.

"Yeah, I think it's going to get us rescued."

"The fire's going to get us rescued?"

"Yeah." I explained to Robbie what I meant.

"Cool," he said. "Then we could ride back to Phoenix in a fire truck. Boy, in one day I will have done more stuff than most kids get to do ever! When I get back to school this fall, and everyone asks me about what I did during the summer, they'll have to give me the whole school year to describe it!"

Suddenly, the wind began to blow real hard. Little loose rocks and grains of sand hurled through the air. I turned on the motor, and rolled the windows up fast. Even with the windows up, I could still feel a sort of gritty sandiness inside the car. Palo Verde trees swayed so hard that it seemed as if they might break, and other pieces of desert plants swirled past them. Soon, it was so dusty that it was impossible to see much of anything through the windows. I didn't think the wind could possibly blow hard enough to knock the car over, but I wasn't absolutely sure of anything anymore. I knew one thing. Wind was certainly going to spread the fire fast. That could make the fire even more visible and bring help faster, or it could mean that no help was coming before we were part of the fire.

There was a loud thud on the car's roof. "What was that?" Robbie called. He clapped his hand across his mouth and whispered, "Do you think there's an animal walking on our car?"

Then there was another thud and another. It didn't really sound like an animal, it almost sounded like . . . I looked out the window. "Robbie, get up off the floor of the car. It's raining. That's rain you hear. Those have to be the biggest drops I've ever seen."

The feeling of grittiness went away as the rain pounded the car. I'd heard the saying about rain coming down in sheets, but I'd never understood it until now. It was so heavy and so thick that you could barely see out the window. It didn't even look like raindrops, just like someone had turned on a giant waterfall. Only a few minutes ago, the desert had seemed to stretch out forever, and now we could only see a few inches beyond the car window. The sounds of rain banged on our car loudly. It sort of felt like we were in a car wash and we'd gotten stuck in it.

The rain was so loud that neither of us said anything. All of a sudden, I felt myself shiver. This was crazy. It had been so hot out, and now I was shivering. I didn't know why. I mean it wasn't that cold in the car, but I looked at Robbie and he was shivering, too. His baseball hat was pulled down low, and I could barely see his face. "You okay?" I practically had to sit right next to him and shout to make myself heard.

He didn't answer, or if he did, I didn't hear him. Finally, he looked up at me, and I could see that his eyes were red. It was too noisy to hear if he was crying, but I could see him sighing deeply. "Well," he shouted in my ear, "at least we won't burn up in the fire!"

I'd almost forgotten about the fire. We hadn't been able to see it or anything else for that matter for quite a while, but I was sure Robbie was right. No fire could withstand this kind of downpour. We could forget about being rescued by any firemen. I tried to make myself feel better by telling myself that even if the fire had burned for longer, and even if the firemen had come to put it out, we really were much too far from it to have ever expected them to find us. Thunder banged and boomed. It felt like the whole desert was shaking. Lightning cracked the sky, and the rain kept pummeling down.

At last, the rain slowed from sheets that you couldn't see through at all to just a normal heavy rainstorm. No wonder people got caught in flash floods! If our car had been in an indented area, it definitely would have been in a river by now. "Well," I said as much to myself as to Robbie, "at least we're not going to get caught in any flash floods!"

"How do you know for sure?" came Robbie's quiet voice.

"Because with as much rain as was out there, we'd have already been in one." I put my head back on the seat and closed my eyes. It was almost nice to listen to the rain, enjoy the cooler temperature, and not worry about any other immediate danger. It was going to be a long, hot, horrible walk tomorrow. We might as well try to enjoy tonight.

"What are you doing?" Robbie looked at me. "Are you sick or something now?"

"No, just relaxing. You ought to try it, too, while you can."

The rain danced gently on the roof, and I was almost lulled to sleep, but something kept bothering me. I couldn't think what it was. I decided that maybe if I quit trying to think about anything, it would pop back into my mind. I stretched a little to make myself more comfortable, and when I put my hand down, it hit something. I opened my eyes to look at it and saw the half-empty gulper next to me. That was it! Get water while I could! I remembered my Scout leader lecturing us before a hike that the greatest danger in the desert was lack of water. Well, here was plenty of water. I just had to get out of the car and get it.

"Robbie, find me all the gulpers, and hurry!" I figured with our luck, just as I'd get organized, the rain would stop.

"Why do you want them? I already found them once,

43

but we put them back under the seat somewhere. I thought we were going to save them until tomorrow. Let's just get them then. I'm too tired to start climbing around the car."

"No, we need them right now!" I started to look for them myself. It was easier than arguing. Robbie shook his head, looked at me as if I were nuts, and pulled a gulper from under one of the seats. Soon, I had all four in front of me. "Take another big drink from one of them right now."

"But I'm not even thirsty!"

I pushed a gulper toward Robbie. "It doesn't matter. We've got to keep drinking stuff. I want to get more liquid in us now, so I can fill this with water for tomorrow."

He drank a few sips. "I can't. It's going to make me puke."

I knew what Robbie meant. Putting the gulper to my own lips, I tasted the sticky-sweet, warm root beer, and I promised myself that once we were out of there, I would never, ever drink root beer again. Yuck! How could I ever have thought this stuff was good? Still, I forced myself to drink as much of it as I could. Then I opened all the gulpers very carefully and poured one into another until I had two full gulpers and two empty ones.

The rain was coming down heavily, but it wasn't terrible, and the sky was actually beginning to get lighter. I opened the car door. "Where are you going?" There was panic in Robbie's voice.

"I'm just gonna get these full of water. I'll be right back."

"Okay," Robbie said to my departing back. "But stay where I can see you . . . uhh, just in case you need help or something."

"Right," I said. "I'll yell if I need anything." I closed the car door and walked a few feet from the car, looking around for a place to wedge the gulpers so that they wouldn't fall over. A bolt of thunder crashed in the air, and I dropped one of the gulpers. "Oh, no!" I shouted to no one. "I can't lose that." But even though I looked carefully in the semi-darkness, the gulper seemed to be gone. It must have wedged under a rock or something. I dropped down onto my hands and knees. The gulper had to be there somewhere! How could something bright yellow just disappear? Then I saw it under a bush. I crawled forward a little and grabbed it. Suddenly, I felt a sharp pain in my knee. I looked down and saw blood coming from it. Geez, it hurt so bad. I wasn't sure if something had bitten me or what. I just wanted to get back to the car, but I knew I had to get the gulpers secured somewhere first. Finally, I wedged one into the space between two small cacti. I managed to scratch my right hand on the cactus needles, but the gulper didn't look as if rain or wind could knock it over. Then I saw three rocks and pushed them together against the other gulper. By now, even though  the rain was not as heavy as it had been, I was pretty well drenched. My hand hurt, and my knee throbbed, but at least we would have water tomorrow, and hopefully, it would be enough.

I opened the car door and fell onto the seat. "Robbie,

see if we have any Kleenex in the back." My knee was bleeding pretty hard, and the blood had started to run down my leg. It kind of made me sick to look at my own blood like that. I forced myself to touch the wound, and felt a piece of something sharp.

Robbie handed me the Kleenex, and I saw his eyes open real big as he looked at my leg. "What . . . what happened out there?"

"Nothing . . . I mean I just cut my leg on a rock. It's no big deal."

I pressed the Kleenex to the cut, and that made it hurt even worse. When I took it away, the blood stopped for a few seconds, and I could see a sharp piece of grey rock sticking in my leg. I knew it had to come out. I tried to put my fingers around the rock and pull, but it hurt so much to even touch the cut, I just couldn't make myself do it.

"Uh, Robbie, I need your help."

Robbie looked at me warily. "With what."

"You gotta get this rock out of my knee."

Robbie shook his head. "Uhh, thanks, but no. It's too gross to reach into your blood."

"Robbie . . ."

"I'm not doin' it."

I sighed deeply. My hand hurt. My knee was throbbing, but I knew when Robbie used that voice that he was not going to do what I wanted without a major fight, and I was too tired for that. What energy I had left had to go to getting the rock out. My knee had to work tomorrow if we were going to be able to walk out of the desert. I gritted my teeth and looked away as I pulled on the rock. "Ahhhh," I screamed, but the rock was still in my knee, and I had caused blood to start flowing faster than ever. I watched it slide down my leg and onto the beige carpet.

I started to reach toward my knee again. I was breathing real hard, and I thought I might puke, when Robbie called, "Wait! Doesn't Mom keep a first-aid kit in the glove compartment?"

"How will that help?" I said with irritation.

Robbie didn't answer. He reached in and pulled out a little white and blue box with a red cross on the top. Inside were bandages and Bactine and a small tweezers. Robbie handed me the tweezers. "Maybe this will make it easier. I'm sorry, Scott; I know it must hurt, but I just can't do it."

I took a deep breath and forced myself to reach toward my knee again. This time the tweezers hung onto the rock and pulled it out. I brought it close to my face, and in the duskiness, I could see how sharp it was, almost like an arrow.

Now, all of a sudden, Robbie wanted to help. He sprayed so much Bactine on my knee that it was running down my leg and over my shorts. "Boy," he said, examining the cut, "that was a lot of blood from such a little cut." Then Robbie sprayed Bactine on my hand and almost got it in my eyes. He started undoing about five Band-Aids.

"That's okay," I stopped him.

"But, I thought you wanted me to help."

I took over and finished covering my knee wound. I was

47

exhausted. My head hurt, my knee hurt, and my hand hurt, but I didn't complain because there was no one to make any of it feel better. I kept thinking of my Scout leader. "Be prepared!" he had always said, but how could anyone be prepared for what we had gone through today? "Never give up," my Scout leader had said. "There's a solution to almost every crisis if you just keep thinking."

"Well, I can't think anymore!" I said almost defiantly. I took off my sopping-wet T-shirt and threw it in the backseat. Now if I could just get those soggy shoes and soaked socks off too. I bent down to try to untie one basketball shoe, and I finally pulled out one foot. Then, holding the basketball shoe for a minute, I got an idea. "Give me your shoes!"

"My shoes? For what?"

"I'm gonna stick them outside the car and let them fill up with water."

"Have you gone nuts?"

"No, and I'm not kidding. Come on, off with your shoes."

Robbie held up his fists. "I'm not letting you fill my shoes with water. No way!"

I sighed. "Robbie, we need to have as much water as we can tomorrow."

"Well I'm not using any water from inside my shoes. Thanks, but I'll pass. I like using glasses to drink from."

I could feel my voice rising angrily. "Robbie, I'd like to be drinking from a glass too. Matter of fact, I'd like to be in the living room right now watching *Star Trek* in the air conditioning, and I'd like to be eating a big bowl of chocolate ice-cream or finishing a pepperoni pizza, then I'd like to climb into my bed tonight, and I'd like to have some ice to put on my knee, but I don't think I'm going to get any of that. Do you?"

Robbie didn't answer, and the frustration of the day kept me yelling at him. "Don't you see that we could die out here without water? We don't have any glasses. The only thing I can see that will hold water is our shoes. Pretty soon, the rain may stop and then it will be too late. That's why you're going to gladly give me your shoes right now, or so help me, I'll rip 'em off your feet!"

obbie didn't say anything to me. He just leaned over and started untying his shoes. When I had both pairs in my hands, I opened the front car door, leaned outside the car, and put the shoes right next to the door. I hoped I was doing the right thing. We had to have water, but we also had to have shoes to walk in the desert. Still, I couldn't exactly imagine anyone stealing our Nike Airs in the middle of nowhere, and they weren't food, so I didn't think any animal might want them. I hoped all my guesses were right.

It rained hard for about another fifteen minutes, and then the rain trickled to a drizzle and stopped. It was actually no darker than when the rain had begun. I guessed that now we were seeing the regular sunset instead of the storm clouds.

Robbie and I were both sitting in the front seat, and Robbie looked at me. "You know, I was supposed to pitch in tonight's game."

"Sorry." I knew Robbie had been anxiously awaiting this game all week. If the team won, they had only one more game to play and then they would win the state title. "You guys probably will lose either way and at least now, they can't blame the loss on your pitching."

Robbie folded his arms across his chest. "Thanks a lot! You just want us to lose because you're not playing."

"That's not true. The coach said that I was a great right-fielder. He just decided to let Tommy Simon play in All-Stars instead of me because he had a better batting average."

"It doesn't matter who plays right field. No one hits there."

"Oh, yeah?" I said. "Just 'cuz you can't hit in that direction doesn't mean a good batter doesn't hit deep into right."

Robbie and I might have kept arguing. We were really good at it since we did it every day of our lives, but we were interrupted by a blood-curdling screech. For a minute both of us froze. Was it the kidnappers? Were they killing someone else? Was it some animal attacking? The shriek sounded again, and this time it sounded as if it were even closer. Robbie grabbed my arm, and clung to it. I looked at the doors to make sure they were locked, and I realized that I had left the door by the shoes unlocked. With Robbie still attached to my arm, I leaned over and pressed the lock.

"Maybe we should get down on the floor," I whispered.

Robbie nodded, but he didn't move. Neither did I. I think we were both just too scared. What if the kidnappers had come back! Then the shriek sounded again, and this time, it seemed as if it were almost on us. Robbie dove for the floor. Another minute, and I was sure some man, animal, or monster would be clawing at our car door.

Then I noticed a small bird nearby. It was hard to believe such a little thing could make so much noise, but as I followed it with my eyes, my ears heard the sound move with it. "Robbie," I said.

"Shh," he whispered. "They'll hear you."

"Robbie, it's just a bird. It's just some little bird over there. Get up and look."

Robbie gingerly rose from the floor of the car and looked at me as if he didn't quite believe me. The bird shrieked a few more times and then flew off into the horizon.

Wiping his hands on his blue T-shirt, Robbie shook his head. "How could such a little thing make such an awful sound? Boy, was I scared! I can't believe it — a bird! Have you ever seen one like it before?"

I shook my head no and said that maybe it only came in the desert. Robbie and I sat silently, and we began to hear more strange noises. I guessed the animals were too hot to come out during the day, but they were starting to be heard now that it was night. In other places, it might have been interesting to try to figure out each noise, but given our situation, each new noise was just another worry to be thought about. We watched as the setting sun cast a pinkish glow to the sky, and then it was dark.

A sliver of the moon provided a little tiny bit of light, and even through the windshield, the stars seemed especially bright, but still, the desert was really, really dark.

It was a different kind of dark than the dark of our room at night. It was a lonely, lost kind of dark.

My knee was throbbing, and I thought it might help if I could stretch it out, so I asked Robbie to get in the backseat. "I think maybe we should just try to go to sleep. We can't do anything tonight, and we want to get started early tomorrow."

Robbie nodded. "I don't really think I can sleep out here. Do you think maybe we could turn the light on in the car?"

I wasn't sure it would work, but it was worth a try. I turned the key and pressed the little black light switch overhead. It didn't exactly make the car light up, but at least Robbie and I could see each other. "I don't think we can keep this light on for too long. We don't want to make the battery run out because we will still need to listen to the radio."

"Maybe we could turn the radio on for just a little while right now. It would probably help us go to sleep."

I knew we should probably wait, but I switched the radio on anyway. There was some talk show on. People were invited to call in and describe their worst day. The first caller was talking about her cat being unable to get out of a tree and her having to call the fire department.

"Boy," I said. "Can you imagine if we could call in?" I pretended to hold a phone to my ear. "Hello. Today was our worst day. You see it started when we got kidnapped and we thought we were going to be killed. We only got to live because the kidnappers decided that it wasn't worth the bullets to kill us. Then we got deserted in the desert. The good news is that we have a car. The bad news is that it ran out of gas. We don't know where we are or exactly how to get out. We don't have any food and we don't have much water. Oh yeah, and we saw a fire and sat through flash-flood warnings and a terrible rainstorm. Other than that, we're having a great day."

Robbie whistled softly. "It doesn't even sound real to me, and I was here for all of it. Boy, when we finally do get home, I wonder if anyone will believe us when we tell them about everything."

The stupid talk show rambled on. Some woman was talking about denting her husband's new car. I snapped off the radio. Dumb people.

I heard Robbie's stomach grumble and I felt my own hunger pains. "Hey, Robbie, if you could have anything to eat right now, what would it be?"

"Hmm, a large pepperoni pizza with extra cheese, and a big cold soda with lots of ice, and then for dessert, probably a double-dip, mint-chocolate ice cream cone."

"I'd have a big juicy cheeseburger and a double order of fries." My mouth was watering at the thought. "Okay, I'm going to turn off the light now and think about that food. Picture us eating tomorrow night, and maybe if we do, we can both go to sleep."

"I'm never gonna be able to sleep out here. In a little while, let's turn the light and the radio back on, okay?"

"Sure, we just have to make sure we can hear the news tomorrow morning about where they're looking for us before we start hiking out of here."

Robbie yawned in spite of himself. "You know, maybe we'll hear that rescuers have spotted our car, and we can just stay right here. The helicopters and the TV stations and everyone will come. I hope they bring lots of good stuff to eat."

I hoped Robbie was right, but I wasn't counting on it.

The light was off for awhile. Eventually, I began to hear Robbie's rhythmic breathing from the backseat. "You asleep?" I whispered, but there was no answer. I envied Robbie. I knew I would need all my strength for tomorrow, but I couldn't go to sleep. My knee hurt every time I turned, and my mind kept wondering if there wasn't some other plan I should be thinking of. Gradually, I began to be aware of another feeling. I had to go to the bathroom. The idea of wandering out into the total darkness was not a good one. *I'll wait,* I told myself. *I don't really have to go.* Pretty soon, I was squirming around the car. This wasn't going to wait until morning. With shaking legs, I started to open the car door.

Robbie stirred in his sleep. "Where 'ya going?" he mumbled.

"To the bathroom." I don't know why I answered

because I was pretty sure Robbie was talking in his sleep.

"Uhhnm, well, don't turn on all the lights."

"Lights!?" I said in frustration. "We don't even have any—," then I stopped myself. The headlights! I could turn on the headlights! I switched the headlights on and in the darkness of the desert night, they gave off a comforting gleam. At least I would be able to see what not to step on. . . . Oops, another little problem. I couldn't walk out into the desert without shoes, and my shoes were outside the car filled with water. Great. We needed the water for tomorrow. I needed the shoes for tonight. I opened the door and looked at the shoes. There was some water in each shoe, but I wouldn't say they were more than a third full, so I poured the water into Robbie's shoes and brought mine into the car. I knew he was going to be ticked tomorrow; he'd say I'd left his full of water on purpose, but I'd have to deal with that then.

I stuck my right foot into my shoe; the shoe felt squishy inside, but what did I expect? I wasn't even going to bother to lace it. Then I picked up my left shoe to put my foot in it, and I felt something slither out of the shoe. I dropped the shoe on the floor and yelled, and I felt the thing slither across my hand.

"What's a matter?" Robbie called.

"Snake," I choked out. "I think there's a snake on me!"

SEVEN

Robbie sat up with a start. "A snake! How'd we get a snake in here?"

No way was I going to sit and explain how I knew there was a snake in the car while it crawled around me somewhere in the dark. It might even be a rattler getting ready to strike. I squirmed, feeling for the door handle. No way I was staying in the car with a snake. "Just get out," I yelled to Robbie. "We gotta get out of the car now."

Both the front and back doors opened at the same time, and we jumped from the car. "Ow," yelled Robbie. "I think I stepped on something." He hobbled to the front of the car and examined the bottom of his sock in the glare of the headlights. "I don't see anything on my foot. I guess the ground was just hard. It wouldn't have hurt if I had my shoes on." Then he looked at me. "Why do you think there's a snake in the car? We've had the windows shut and the doors locked. Maybe you were just dreaming."

"Well, not exactly . . ."

"Yeah, well what exactly then?" Robbie looked part asleep, part confused, and part mad. "Well . . ."

"Well, I had to go to the bathroom."

"Yeah, and . . ."

"And well . . . I went to put on my shoes, so I could go out a little ways into the desert."

"I thought we were supposed to leave our shoes outside for them to get water. What'd you do with the water that was in your shoes?"

"I put it in yours."

"Oh, thanks a lot!"

"Robbie!" I shouted. There was silence in the desert night as the two of us glared at each other. But then I decided that maybe if I went over exactly how the snake got in the car, I could think how to get it out, so I said, "I got one shoe on, see," and I pointed to my foot to show him it wasn't just my imagination. "Then I went to put the other one on. Everything happened so fast from there, but I think when I bent down to pick up my other shoe from the ground, a little field mouse ran onto it. And then suddenly, I thought I saw this big snake coming at my shoe from under the car. Then part of it rose up off the ground and the whole thing slithered into the car real fast. That's when I screamed and told you to get out."

Robbie looked at me for a minute, and then he bit his lip. "Okay, if you think that's what happened, then I guess we better find out."

We decided to walk back to the car door and open

it. That way the inside light would go on and then maybe we could at least see the snake. I put my hand on the door handle and took a deep breath. Everything had happened so fast with the mouse and my shoe that I wasn't sure if

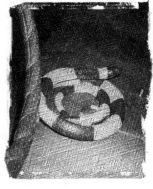

we'd see nothing, or if a big, poisonous snake would spring at us.

I opened the driver's car door and jumped back just in case the snake was ready to strike. Robbie stared through the passenger side window onto the now-lighted seat. "Holey moley, there's a big snake on our front seat."

"That's what I've been trying to tell you," I shouted, slamming the door shut again.

"I can't believe it," Robbie said over and over again.

"I told you it was there."

"Scott, we gotta do something. There's a snake sitting on the front seat of the car, and we're out here where there's probably a zillion other snakes just waiting to bite us or squeeze us or something." He looked sort of glassy-eyed. "What are we gonna do?"

I ran my hand through my hair. I didn't know what we were going to do. I didn't want to stay out here all night any more than Robbie did. There were lots of strange noises, and all we could see was the path lighted by the headlights. Who knew what was out there in the darkness just beyond the headlights?

"I've got an idea," Robbie said. "Why don't we turn the radio on real loud and leave the car door open? Maybe that will bother the snake's ears so much that it will crawl away from the music."

I looked at my little brother. "I don't think snakes have ears!"

"You got a better idea?"

There was a loud hooting sound in the distance and Robbie and I both jumped. "Okay, we'll try it," I said. I didn't think it would work, but I didn't have any better plan. We crept back to the car door and stared into the window, but without the interior light on, it was too hard to see anything. "So, uh, you want to open the door this time?" I said. After all, Robbie was always complaining that I took over just because I was older.

"Okay," he said. "And then you reach in and turn on the radio. And be really careful, because when we looked before, the snake was curled up on the seat right next to the radio."

"I dunno, Robbie. What if the snake is still right there? I don't think I could get my hand away if it started to strike."

Robbie sighed. "Maybe it isn't such a great plan."

Robbie and I looked at each other, each of us feeling fear and frustration. Finally, I said, "Why don't we at least open the car door and see where the snake is? Maybe it moved away from the radio."

Of course, we had no idea what to do if the snake was

still right by the radio, but there didn't seem to be any other thing to do except open the car door and see where the snake was. I put my hand on the doorknob, took a deep breath, threw open the door and jumped back in case the snake was right there. Robbie jumped too, and we almost tripped over each other. No snake emerged from the car, and keeping the open door carefully in our sight at all times, we walked back toward the car. With the light on inside, it was plain to see that the snake hadn't moved. It was big and it had black, whitish-yellow, and dark red on it. Robbie whispered, "Is that a rattler?"

"I don't think so," I whispered back; "but it could be. I don't want to find out. It doesn't look very friendly."

We decided it was just too dangerous to try for the radio, and besides, we didn't know if snakes really moved away from music or not. We climbed up on the hood of the car and sat down. That way we could stare through the front window at the snake and see if it crawled out. Meanwhile, we'd be off the ground in case the snake had any friends slithering around looking for it.

Robbie's and my eyes glared through the windshield at the snake. If eye power could have moved it, that snake would have been gone. Instead, it seemed perfectly content to be coiled up on the front seat of the car, and why not? The car seat was a lot more comfortable than the hard metal hood we were sitting on. I looked up at the sky. The stars were so bright. I could easily see both the big and the little dipper. I'd once read a book about a guy who used the stars to guide him, and I wished I could remember how he'd done it.

After a while, my rear hurt from sitting on the hood. Robbie said he was more tired than he'd ever been in his whole life, but he didn't plan to sleep until we could get back into a locked car. That worried me. I knew that we were going to have a really hard day tomorrow. We needed all our strength, and that meant we needed to sleep some tonight. But how to get the snake out and us into the car, I just didn't know. "What's that?" Robbie whispered.

There was a strange noise off to the right. "Probably nothing," I whispered back.

"What kind of nothing makes that kind of noise?"

"I don't know."

Robbie wrapped his arms around himself. "Scott, we gotta get back in the car. We really do."

I thought and thought until I thought my brain would burst. "Okay, I got it. We'll get the jack out of the car. Since it's strong enough to hold up the car, it ought to be strong enough to kill a snake, right?" I was beginning to feel my heart pump. Now this was a plan that could work.

"I'll take the jack, and I'll hit the snake. Then the snake will be dead, and I'll use the jack to push it out of the car." I raised an eyebrow. "Pretty good idea, huh?"

Robbie looked at me. "I think it's a great idea. Really. I think it was so smart of you to think of, but . . . Now, don't get mad or anything. I'm not saying this to be mean. But I think I should be the one to hit the snake."

"You?"

"Yeah, in baseball, you miss so much of the time. Scott, we can't strike out when it comes to the snake."

I started to say something mean back to him, sort of reflex action, but I had to admit that he was right about whose aim was better. Robbie was the leading hitter on the baseball team; he was better than a lot of the older guys. Still, I thought I should be the one to take the risk with the snake. After all, I was the older brother. I went around to the back of the station wagon. I was pretty sure that when Robbie saw how heavy a jack was, he'd change his mind about who should use it.

We climbed over the roof of the car and leaned over the back of it. I grabbed the station wagon's back door handle. Swinging the door open, we peered upside down into the back of the car. "Uh, Robbie, you know where the jack is?"

"Nope, I don't think I've ever seen a jack except on TV when I saw guys fixing flat tires."

Truthfully, that was the only place I'd ever seen one, too. On TV they'd just opened the trunk of the car and there'd been a spare tire and a jack. The only problem with that was that a station wagon didn't have a trunk. Maybe a station wagon didn't have a spare tire or a jack, either. I began to get a sinking feeling, but I didn't give up. Much as I hated to, I climbed off the car. Standing on the ground, I stared again into the back of the station wagon. There was a third seat that could be pulled up out of storage space in the back, and I released the levers and pulled, hoping to see a jack. I looked in the wells in the back, but zip. Nothing. No jack.

I rubbed my eyes. Why couldn't anything go right? "Come on, Robbie, let's climb back on the hood of the car, and we'll try to think of something else." When we were sitting on the car and staring through the windshield, we could easily see the snake on the front seat. It was creepy looking.

The headlights didn't seem as bright to me as they were before, and I began to worry that if we didn't think of something pretty soon, we were going to be sitting out here on the hood of the car in pitch black darkness. Staring ahead, I could see a small Palo Verde tree in the headlights. "Robbie," I said slowly, thinking as I spoke, "See that tree over there? I'm going to go get a branch off of it, and we'll use the branch to push the snake out of the car."

"Okay," Robbie said wearily.

I had only one shoe on. My other foot was barefoot. I had been walking around the car very carefully, but the Palo Verde tree was a ways away. I couldn't risk getting cactus stickers in my foot, so I decided I would have to hop to the Palo Verde tree. I was really sorry that I'd ever taken off my basketball shoes in the first place. It was a dumb idea. By tomorrow, whatever water they'd gathered would probably have soaked into the shoes anyway.

As I got a little ways away from the car, the sounds of

the desert seemed even more threatening. I made myself keep hopping because I knew that if I really stopped to listen, I'd run right back to the car. Finally, I'd hopped to the Joshua tree. It was a scraggly little thing, and the branches were pretty puny. I wished I'd had my Boy Scout knife to cut one off, but it was sitting at home next to my bed on my nightstand. I leaned down and cleared a spot so that I could put both feet down. It felt great to stand on two feet, but I worried a lot about my bare foot. I knew there were scorpions and all kinds of other yucky bugs out there, and I hoped my bare foot wouldn't make a tempting target.

I found the smallest long branch on the tree, and I began to twist it back and forth, then up and down. I was panting with effort, and the dumb branch still clung to the tree. The next thing I knew something was coming up behind me. I jumped around, screamed, and made a fist. I might only have one punch, but whatever it was, I'd give it my best shot before it attacked.

"Don't hit—it's me. It's just me!" Robbie yelled.

My heart was pounding a million miles an hour. "What—what are you doing here?" I gasped. "You scared me to death!"

"Sorry. While I was sitting on the hood, I saw something gleaming in the headlights. I got off the car to see what it was, and guess what—it was a tin can. I took my shoes, poured the water from my shoes into the can, and look, I'm here! Of course, my shoes are a gross mess, but at least I have 'em on, and we still have the water." Robbie looked proud of himself. I was proud of him too, and I told him so. Maybe I didn't give my little brother enough credit.

Together, we worked on the tree branch. It certainly didn't want to leave that tree. Finally, we got it free, and we headed back to the car. I held on to Robbie's shoulder as I hopped my way back. When we reached the car, we approached the open door very carefully. A first glance told us that the snake wasn't still on the seat, and almost in unison, Robbie and I looked down at our feet to make sure nothing was slithering toward us. Then we noticed the snake. It was still in the car; it had just moved to the floor.

"Exactly how are we gonna do this?" Robbie whispered. "That branch isn't very heavy. If we hit the snake with it, he might just get mad instead of dead."

I looked at the snake. It couldn't possibly have grown since we'd been out getting the branch. It must have just spread out a little more. I gulped. "I guess we're just going to have to use the stick to shove him out." My throat felt real dry. My hands were shaking so much that I held the branch with both hands. "Go around and open the other door, then come back over here. We'll stand here behind him, and we'll shove him out the driver's side door. I leaned into the car on the passenger side, and I noticed that the beige part of the snake almost blended in with the beige carpet on the floor. I heard Robbie take a sharp breath, and then I heard a ringing in my ears as I edged the branch closer and closer to the snake. I felt like I might pass out. The ringing got louder, and then I felt the stick touch the snake. It took all the willpower I had not to scream and pull the stick away. Instead, I made myself put the stick next to the middle of the snake, and then I pushed as hard as I could toward the open door. There was a hissing sound.

You did it!" Robbie squealed. "The snake's out. Quick, let's get in." My breath was coming in hard pants, but I dropped the branch and jumped in the car. Robbie and I pulled the doors shut, and I sank back in the seat. I was shaking all over. "We did it! We did it!" Robbie exclaimed. "Boy, I wish I could have kept the snake's skin. That would have really been something to show people."

I was still in shock. I didn't care about the snakeskin. I was just glad it was out of the car, and we were in it! Robbie got up on his knees and pressed his face to the glass of the front windshield. "What are you doing?" I asked.

"I'm looking to see if I can see the snake crawling away. I want to know just how big it really was so I can tell all my friends."

I put my hand over my face and closed my eyes. Let Robbie look all he wanted. I don't think he realized how dangerous the snake could have been. I mean what if I'd pushed one way, and it had sprung out and struck the other? I shuddered thinking of that huge snake coiling itself around my arm. With my eyes closed, I could almost see it moving up my arm, so I quickly opened them and sat up. Robbie's face was still pressed to the windshield. "Well, you see him?"

"Nope," Robbie sounded disappointed.

"I think we better turn off the headlights. We don't want to use up the battery before tomorrow morning. We've got to be able to hear the news then."

I reached to shut off the headlights, and Robbie groaned, "I like it a lot better with some light. Exactly what is it that uses up a battery anyway?"

"I don't know. I can't know everything. I just know that if the car isn't running and you leave the lights or the radio on for too long the battery goes dead." I was tired, and I was grumpy. "I don't have any idea how long is too long. I do remember the time you didn't shut the door all the way and the light in the car stayed on all night, and in the morning, Mom had a dead battery. Remember? She had to call Triple-A to come jump start the car, and she was late for work, and we were late for school? That's all I know about batteries."

"Okay, you don't have to take my head off. I just wondered. It sure is dark out here. Did you hear that noise?"

I didn't answer. I heard lots of noises, but the snake had worn me out. I just wanted to sink into this seat and not listen. It felt so good just to sit there that I wasn't sure I was ever going to get up. Unfortunately, it only took a few minutes to make me change my mind. I remembered what had started the whole snake situation as I felt an overwhelming need to go to the bathroom. I'd been so scared that I guess I'd forgotten before, but now I definitely needed to go. I tried to tell myself just not to think about it because there was no way I wanted to get out of this car until it was light, but the harder I tried to think about something else, the more I could only think about getting out of there and going to the bathroom. I grimaced. This wasn't going to wait until morning no matter how much I wanted it to. I reached over and turned on the headlights.

Robbie sat up from the backseat. "Hey, I thought you just said we had to keep them off."

"Yeah, well, I have to go to the bathroom."

"Oh. Can't you wait 'til morning?"

"No."

"Well I'm sure that the snake must have crawled far away from here by now." I think Robbie was trying to be helpful. It didn't help. "Besides, when I asked you before, you said snakes didn't come out when you peed."

It seemed like it must have been years ago that I'd said that to Robbie instead of a few hours ago; besides, it was a lie. I didn't know anything about the subject. That was the problem with school. They didn't teach you the stuff you really needed to know. Suddenly, I had an idea. "I'm not getting off the car."

Robbie yelped, "Yeah, well you're not going in here. That's just too gross."

I opened the door to the car, climbed out and onto the hood, stood up, and took care of business. Feeling much better, I climbed back into the car. Everything out there wore a person out. Even going to the bathroom couldn't be simple. I was just about to reach out and turn off the lights again when a coyote ran in front of the car and grabbed a squealing rabbit. The coyote tore at the rabbit, and Robbie and I sat frozen. Blood spurted from the rabbit as the coyote ran off with it. "Geez," Robbie finally whispered, "you could have been right out there going to the bathroom. I . . . uh . . . I don't think we ought to get out of the car again until it's light out, okay?"

It sounded like a good idea to me. Both of us sat thinking about the bloody rabbit and the coyote. Then Robbie leaned over the seat and turned on the radio. "I know you said we gotta save the battery, but I just need to hear some people's voices, some regular old ordinary life stuff. Please?" Robbie's face looked real white.

"Okay," I said. Actually, the idea sounded pretty good to me too, and we wouldn't keep the radio on too long.

The only station that would come in was a golden oldies station, but at least it was something. "And now for your K-O-O-L news of the hour," blared the radio. "It's one A.M. on this Thursday morning." First the announcer told about a fire that had broken out in a large Phoenix building. Then he talked about the monsoon-like rainstorm that had hit the Valley. He mentioned a couple of

71

other stories, and then he broke for a commercial. "Boy, do you think they already forgot about us?" Robbie asked.

"Of course not," I said, but I was a little worried myself. Why hadn't they said anything about us? Did that mean there was no search going on? The radio announcer continued with other stories. The news was almost over, and I was biting my lip in nervousness. Mom wouldn't let them just forget about us. "And finally," said the announcer, "there's been no further word on the two missing Phoenix boys. Police say there has been no ransom demand. Again, we are asking anyone who has seen a cream-colored Chevy Caprice station wagon, license CCJ-023, to please contact Crime Stop immediately."

I wanted to yell at the radio guy. I wanted to scream at him that no one could see our license plate. We were stuck out in the middle of the desert in pitch black darkness. I knew it wouldn't do any good to scream at a radio, so I forced myself to say, "See, Robbie, they're still looking for us."

"Yeah, which means they don't have any idea where we are."

With that discouraging thought, we listened to a couple more songs, and then we agreed that we better turn off the radio to save the battery. I said, "Maybe tomorrow morning, we'll hear that they've found out we're here, and they're on their way to rescue us. Meanwhile, we've gotta try to sleep so we can think tomorrow."

Robbie stretched out in the backseat, and I lay down

in front. We took the clothes Mom had bought and wadded them up to make pillows. It wasn't anything like being home in bed, but it sure beat being out on the hood of the car. My whole body hurt. My eyes felt scratchy under my eyelids, and my knee throbbed. I knew that I had to sleep, but as tired as I was, I just couldn't make my eyes stay closed. Pretty soon, I could hear Robbie snoring in the backseat. Finally, just as I had about given up on sleeping, I felt myself drifting off.

"No, no, don't kill me," Robbie screamed at the top of his voice. "Please just don't kill me!" I forced my eyes open. My heart hammered. The kidnappers must have come back! They had Robbie. I made myself sit up. I didn't know what I could do, but I couldn't just let them take my little brother.

"Leave him alone!" I screamed, trying to make my eyes focus in the darkness.

"What? What is it?" Robbie yelled. "Scott, answer me. Who's hurting you? What's wrong?"

My heart was still hammering. "Are you there by yourself?"

"Yeah, aren't you?" There was a strong note of fear in Robbie's voice.

"But you screamed that you were being killed."

"I did?" Robbie asked. "I don't think I screamed."

I put my head in my hands. "You must have been having a nightmare."

Robbie reached out and put his hand on my shoulder.

"I think I was just sleeping. Maybe you were having a nightmare. Hey, it's going to be light out pretty soon. Let's just turn on the radio for a few minutes. That'll help."

Soon light shone, both inside and in front of the car, but it was much dimmer than it had been. I knew we couldn't keep the lights or the radio on for very long. The battery must be starting to go. It helped a little to have the rock-n-roll oldies blaring from the radio, but it was depressing to have the announcer sounding as if the whole world was just great. The blue glow from the radio clock showed 3:17. I wondered how soon it would get light.

"Hey, remember this song?" Robbie began to snap his fingers. "You and Howard Langson did a lip sync to it in the school talent show last year. You wore that crazy green-haired wig, and everybody loved your act."

"You know, we *did* use that song." I hadn't even remembered when I'd heard it on the radio. But now that I'd been reminded I could see myself and Howard on stage. It had been lots of fun. "That green wig was really something. I wonder what happened to it." I could see me and Howard getting our costumes together. "We got two cans of fluorescent green paint, and his mom's old wig looked real different when we were through with it. Only problem was that Howard sort of forgot to ask his mom before we painted it. Boy, was he in trouble. Then after she saw the show, his mom decided that our act was worth her wig."

I grinned, remembering. "Hey, Robbie, you ought to try out for the talent show this year. You'll be old enough."

"Nah, I don't think so; nobody could top your act from last year."

"You really think so?" I couldn't believe this was coming from Robbie, who never said anything nice about anything I did.

"Yeah, everyone laughed. I mean, even the sixth-graders who thought they were the only funny ones. Boy, that night, I told everyone around me that the guy on the left was my brother."

"You did?" I was amazed. "But you never said anything about it to me."

"Oh right, I was supposed to be like Mom and run up saying how proud I was of you, and that you were adorable." Robbie put his finger in his mouth and made a gagging sound. "Give me a break."

Imagine that, I thought, Robbie actually telling people, kids at school even, that he thought I was good. Before I could say anything else, the radio announcer came on saying that it was time for another news update. The newscaster talked about the fire again. He said that the storm had knocked down a power pole in west Phoenix, and that service to the area might not be restored until the morning. Then he said, "Searching continues for two boys kidnapped at the 32nd street Mini-Mart yesterday afternoon. Police have been following every lead. Some witnesses reported seeing the car in Flagstaff and others reported the car at the opposite end of the state in Nogales. Authorities do not know if the boys are still in that car or if they are still alive, nor is there any word as to why they were taken. We'll update you as we get new information. Meanwhile, the search continues, and police are asking everyone to watch for a Chevy Caprice station wagon—"

Robbie turned off the radio and banged at the light switch, plunging us into darkness. "Nobody's ever gonna find us!"

He sounded awful. "Hey," I said, "that's why we're going to go find them. Remember? We're going to be TV stars. We can't do that if we just wait around here forever to be rescued." Robbie didn't say anything, so I said, "Rob, really, somehow, it's all going to be okay."

He sighed. "Yeah, I guess we've been doing pretty good so far. We got rid of the kidnappers and the snake."

It was funny in a sad sort of way. I was trying to make Robbie feel better, and I think he was trying to do the same for me, but both of us were scared to death about what the morning might bring.

There was silence in the car, mostly because I think neither one of us could think of anything good to say. We each stretched out on our own seat, and with a mixture of a little hope and a lot of fear, we waited for the sky to get light.

I turned and twisted on the seat, trying to find a comfortable position. "Go to sleep," I ordered myself, but sleep would not come. I'd close my eyes and see that snake on the kidnapper's hand, or I'd hear the guy named Slam say, "You want to kill 'em?" I guess Robbie must have been having the same problem because I'd hear his light snoring for a few minutes, and then he would move around the seat. I sighed. There was nothing I could do to make myself any less scared, but maybe I could say something to help Robbie sleep and make the night pass. "Hey, guy," I teased. "If you don't sleep, you're gonna have big, black bags under your eyes tomorrow, and when we go on TV, people are all going to say, 'Isn't it amazing that they're brothers! The dark-haired one is awesome looking, and the other one is just plain ugly.'"

"Ha," Robbie said, rising to the bait. "Even with the biggest circles in the world, I'd still look better than you."

"No way!" I said.

"Yeah way, easy way!" Then the tone of Robbie's voice changed. "Scott, no kidding now, do you really think we're going to make it out of here? Do you really think we'll get home to be on TV?"

"Of course! Don't be dumb! Nothing's going to happen to us. We've got to be okay to be on television." I didn't believe my own words. In fact, I was going over and over what to do when it did get light. I wished I were one year older. Then maybe I would have finished a wilderness survival badge, and I'd have known what to do instead of just guessing. There was this TV game show on called *Wheel of Fortune.* I sort of felt like I was spinning that wheel. Only instead of a spot marked *bankrupt* where you lost your money, our wrong spin meant we lost our lives.

My mind raced. I kept hoping that when we turned on the radio when it got light, we'd hear something about searchers being in the desert, or maybe we'd even see them, but I didn't think that was going to happen. Would we have to hike out of here? If only I had some idea how far we were from the road. At least, when we walked, we could follow the tire tracks.

Finally, the first rays of light came. It was still way too dark to wake Robbie, but I noticed that it had gotten very quiet. I had this crazy picture in my mind that it was time for all the night shift sounds or animals to go to sleep, and the day shift hadn't awakened yet. The sun broke a little more, and long shadows of saguaro cacti stretched out along the desert. I saw a cactus wren swoop on top of a cactus near our car and begin its ratchety song.

Robbie sat up with a start. "Scott, watch out, a machine gun. I heard it!"

I leaned over the seat. "It's okay, Rob. See that bird up there? The one with the big dark spot on its front? That's what's making the machine-gun sound. Listen."

The bird "sang" again. "That's the ugliest bird call I ever heard!" Robbie exclaimed. "How'd you know that's what was making the sound?"

"Two reasons. First, I was watching it this morning, and I saw it. Second, when we went camping in Scouts this spring, we heard a whole bunch of cactus wrens early in the morning. Most of us were up when the racket started, but Jose Sanchez was still sleeping. It was pretty funny. He jumped out of his sleeping bag and started screaming that we were being attacked by guns. So you see, you're not the only one to be fooled."

Robbie looked at me doubtfully. I continued. "Anyway, it's just as well that you're up. I was just about to wake you for our morning news broadcast and our delicious breakfast of red Lifesavers and warm root beer."

"Yuck, breakfast sounds gross." Robbie rubbed his eyes. "Geez, I really didn't think I could sleep out here, but I guess I did."

I dug around the seat for the gulpers of root beer and opened the Lifesavers. The Lifesavers weren't too bad, but the root beer was flat and warm and all around pretty awful. I decided I'd save it for later. Right now, it didn't seem all that hot, and I wasn't that thirsty. I guess some little part of me kept hoping that rescuers would come pretty soon and keep us from having to drink the flat root beer.

"Well, Robbie," I said, feeling my stomach churn. "Now that we've had that great breakfast, are you ready for the morning news?"

"Yeah, I guess so. I wish I could be that announcer on the radio. I know just what I'd say." He pretended to hold a microphone to his face. "The sheriff's rescue unit has located the missing Ratliffe boys, and we'll have live coverage of their rescue." Robbie took a breath. "You know, it'd be really neat if the guys from the TV show *Rescue 911* were with the sheriff, and they made a show out of our rescue."

"Right," I said. At this point, I didn't care about the TV stations; I didn't care about being famous. Well, maybe I cared a little. Mostly, I just wanted to hear someone say they knew right where we were and then promise we were going to be rescued soon. I reached out to turn the silver knob on the radio marked *power,* and I saw that my fingers were shaking. What if we turned on the radio, and the news didn't say anything at all about us? What if they'd already given up? It was too awful to think about, so I forced my fingers to turn the switch.

"Hey," Robbie said, "I thought you were going to turn on the radio."

I turned the switch harder until the volume was up

all the way, but the car stayed silent. "Oh, no," I groaned, slamming the dashboard with my hand.

"What . . . what is it?"

"The battery must be dead. The radio won't come on."

Robbie pushed his baseball hat up on his head. "Then how are we ever going to hear about how the rescue's coming? How are we gonna know whether to stay here or try to walk to the highway?"

"Would you quit asking questions!" I shouted. I couldn't look at Robbie. I ran my finger around the steering wheel, wishing the car could somehow magically start. It was beginning to get very warm in there, and I knew we would have to make some decisions soon. The last report we had heard on the radio had basically said that no one knew where we were. If we stayed in our car and no rescuers were looking in this part of the desert, we'd die from the heat before being found. If we walked back to the road, it would be long and hot and we wouldn't have shade, but at least there would be some cars once we got there, and we would get rescued. I explained everything to Robbie. "I'm going to go get the gulpers I left out in the rain last night. We're going to need all the liquids we can get." I didn't tell him that I didn't know if the gulpers were even still there or if they had any water in them at all.

"Well," Robbie said, "at least I saved this can of water from our shoes." He held it out, and we both looked at the water inside. "Kinda gross, huh?" Robbie said.

Kinda wasn't even the word for it. The water was a greyish-brown color. I guess that was no surprise. The insides of both Robbie's and my shoes were pretty disgusting, and that's where the water had been. "Well, we don't have to drink that," I said. "We can just use it to cool off or something."

"Uh-huh," Robbie said, sounding as if he didn't plan to let that water get anywhere near him. "The stuff in the gulpers better not look the same way."

I got out of the car to check them and found the first good news of the morning. The gulpers were still right where I had wedged them, and the water inside looked fine. Each one was almost a fourth-full, and I poured one into the other so that we wouldn't have to carry any unnecessary stuff. My hand shook as I poured because I was trying to be so careful not to spill even one drop. It was hard to believe that it had rained so much last night because the ground under me looked as if it hadn't had rain in years. I don't know where all the rain in a desert went, but it certainly didn't stay around. I walked back to the car with the gulper of water and held it out toward Robbie. "Great news. This water is even clear, like regular water!"

I climbed back in the front seat of the car. It was time to think of a plan and get out of there. "I'm gonna sit here and try to decide what we should take with us. We want to take whatever might help us or keep us cool, but we don't want to carry anything extra." I was really talking to myself more than Robbie. "It's going to be hot and a long way to the main streets. We don't want to get too tired to get there."

Then I turned toward him. "Tell you what, while I look around the car, why don't you scout out the tracks a little way ahead. That way we'll know where we're headed. When you get back, we'll take a little drink of water, grab our gear, and get out of here!"

Robbie opened the car door. "Right on, Robbie the amazing tracker to the rescue." He seemed glad to be doing something useful. I started thinking of what we would need. Robbie had his baseball cap, which was good, but I probably needed to figure out something to cover my head. Then I'd have to see if there was some way to hook the gulpers onto something so we didn't have to carry them in our hands the whole way. I got out of the car to search the back of the station wagon, and just as I opened the back door, I heard Robbie scream.

Oh God, I thought, *what now?* "Robbie! Robbie!" I yelled. But there was no answer from Robbie except another scream and then silence. I grabbed the branch we'd used against the snake. It wasn't much of a weapon, but it would have to do. Then I ran to face whatever the terrible thing was.

When I got around the front of the car, I could see Robbie kneeling on the ground. There was no other person or animal around him. "Robbie," I yelled, coming toward him. "What's wrong. Did you fall? Did you get bitten by something?"

Robbie still didn't answer, and as I got closer to him,

I could see a sort of glassy look in his eyes. "Robbie," I shouted, "you tell me what's wrong this minute!"

"Wrong? Wrong?" Robbie asked in a high-pitched, unnatural voice when I was right in front of him. "Scott, do you see any tire tracks? How can we follow the tracks out of the desert when there aren't any tracks to follow?"

It couldn't be. This was impossible. The tracks had to be there. I ran ahead of Robbie. After all, tracks didn't just disappear overnight. They had been there last night when we ran out of gas. We hadn't moved the car, so where were the tracks? I ran faster away from the car. Maybe they were just a little ways up. The car tracks were our only chance to know which way was out.

Totally out of breath, I sank down into the dirt. Robbie was right; there were no tracks. Then the reason hit me. The storm. There had been so much wind, so much blowing dust, and then so much heavy rain. The tracks had either been blown or rained away or both. It didn't much matter. What mattered was that our only road map out of here had been wiped out. I put my hand above my eyes to shade them from the glaring sun and looked out across the desert. For as far as I could see, there were only cacti and rocks. One direction didn't look any different from another. There were some scrawny dirt paths that went off in different ways at different places, but there was no way to know if we should follow one of them.

I continued to sit in the dirt. I noticed that my new, blue baggy shorts were torn in the knee and filthy. I wiped my runny nose across the shoulder of what had been my favorite white T-shirt when things like that mattered.

I had to face the truth, and the truth was that no car tracks meant that we had no chance. We'd tried so hard, but trying hadn't been enough. I sat there feeling the burning sun and wondered what it would be like to be dead. I thought maybe I should just tell Robbie to come back to the car with me, and we'd lie down and go to sleep. Maybe we'd be dead without ever waking up; then it wouldn't hurt so bad to die. My legs felt so heavy; I couldn't make them stand up. *In a minute,* I thought; *in a minute.*

Suddenly, something was tugging at me. "See, I told you the tracks were gone. Why are you just sitting there? What are we gonna do, huh? What are we gonna do?"

"I don't know, and I don't care!" I said. I could taste the tears running down my cheeks. "Why don't you just go figure it out for yourself?"

In a very small voice, Robbie said, "Okay, I'll try." He leaned over. "Hey, you want to wear my baseball hat for a while? It always makes me feel better."

I looked at my little brother. He was a pretty sturdy kid, but he looked real young and real scared. That baseball hat was the most special thing he owned. All I had to do to start a fight with him was to touch it. From the beginning of second grade, when his best friend had gone to St. Louis and brought it back from a Cardinals' game, that hat hadn't been out of his sight. Now he was offering it to me.

"Scott, 'member Coach in the Dodger game? We were

down by eight runs at the bottom of the sixth, and everyone wanted to just get the game over and go home. 'Member what coach said?"

I remembered. How could I forget that huge guy standing over us, chomping gum and saying angrily, "I can't stand a quitter. Anyone who gives up now is off the team. What's the matter with you guys anyway? You think life was meant to be easy? You think you're just supposed to win? Ha! Life's tough. You be tougher. You get out there on that field, and you play every minute like you're winners. Got it? We lose—well then we lose. You quit fighting every minute to win, and you better not even come back to the dugout because you're not part of my team."

Robbie was staring at me and biting his lip. "Well, do you remember? He said—"

I interrupted. "I remember. Okay, so we won't quit, but I don't see how we're gonna get a home run."

We decided that there was no point to walking since we had no idea where to walk. We'd just have to stay with the car and hope someone found us. It would be easier to spot it than to spot two kids wandering nowhere. It seemed like a long walk back to the car, but once we got there, I decided that I'd promised Robbie I wasn't going to quit, and I'd do my best not to.

"Okay, first thing is that I gotta try to remember what it said in my Scout badge book about wilderness survival." Little bits started coming back to me. "We have to try not to sweat."

Robbie looked disgusted. "Geez, we're lost in a huge desert with no one around, and you're worrying about not smelling. You think Jennifer Watkins is going to come with the rescue people?" He tried to imitate her voice. Are you afraid she'll say, 'Oh, Scott, I'm glad you're safe, but you smell too bad for me to kiss.'"

I smiled in spite of myself. "I do not like Jennifer

Watkins. How many times have I told you that? I just think she—"

"You just think she should be your girlfriend."

"Wrong about that and way wrong about why we can't sweat. It doesn't have to do with Jennifer. The survival book said that to stay alive in the desert you can't get dehydrated." I sighed, "If we had lots of water, that would be easy. Since we don't, I'm not sure what we'll do."

"Right now, I think I'd rather have air conditioning than water. Boy, that sun is hot." He wiped his forehead. "I wish we at least had a little shade. Let's get in the car."

"We can't stay in the car. It'll be too hot."

"It can't be hotter."

I was too tired to argue with him. "Get in," I said, shrugging.

"I will," he replied defiantly.

It didn't take Robbie long to get out of the car again. "Okay, you're right, but why?"

"Remember all those warnings on TV about not leaving your dog in the car in the summer because when it's a hundred degrees outside, it can be a hundred and thirty in the car?"

"Great," Robbie said. "The car is the only shade we have for as far as we can see, and we can't use it. What are we supposed to do, make shade?"

"That's it, Robbie!" I shouted. "You're brilliant."

"I am?" He looked confused.

"Yeah, that's what we have to do. We have to make shade."

"Uh-huh, make shade. Scott, I was only kidding. It's not exactly like we can grow a tree right here. We don't have any way to make it shady. I mean, we could ask the sun to set early today, but I don't think it would."

I walked over to the car and pulled open the door. "We need to start looking at every single thing in this car to see how it could help us. Let's start with the backseat."

"Geez, it's hot in here," Robbie said.

"Yeah, well, grab anything you see, and we'll get out."

"Look," Robbie said, pulling a big, white beach towel from under the seat. "And I think there's another one jammed in here." We climbed out of the car with two big white beach towels.

"So . . . what do we do with them?" Robbie asked.

I looked at them carefully and stared at the desert around us. My eyes stopped on two large saguaros off to the right that were real close together. "Robbie, get the towels. I've got an idea." I walked over to the cacti and heaved one towel up toward it. The towel fell to the ground. "Darn!" I said. I picked it up and tossed it again. This time the end of the towel caught on some of the needles on one of the arms of the cactus. Then I took the end of the towel still dangling on the ground and tossed it at the other cactus until it had caught, too. "Look, we have shade!" I said proudly.

Robbie came over to stand under the towel. "Wow," he said. "Let's see what else is in the car!" We returned to the car and pulled out everything we could find onto the ground next to the hood. It wasn't long before we had quite a pile. "I never knew our car had so much junk," Robbie exclaimed.

"Good thing," I answered. "We're going to have to turn it into our survival gear." We had gotten two carpeted floor mats from the floor of the front seat and a seat cushion from the driver's seat. We had also found two unwrapped cookies that had been wedged under the front seat, part of one roll of Lifesavers, a sharp tool to pry off hubcaps, a pad of paper and a pencil, and all the packages that Mom had bought at the mall. Also, while tearing through the car, we'd finally located the jack and the spare tire. They too were now on the ground.

I looked at everything, and I wondered how to use it all. I opened one of the bags and the white skirt and blouse that Mom had bought tumbled onto the ground. I picked them up and threw the skirt at Robbie. "Put this on."

"No way," Robbie squealed. "Get serious."

"I am serious. It's like the camel drivers in the movies. Remember, they always wore those white head things and long white robes? This is the closest we've got."

"Uh-huh, how come you aren't wearing a skirt?"

"Because you're my little brother, and we only have one skirt. I'm trying to help you."

"It's okay, Scott. You go ahead and take it. In fact, you know how Mom always complains that we don't share enough? Well, I really want you to get to wear this skirt." Robbie grinned.

"Okay, fine, I will." I stared at the skirt for a minute and pulled it on. It reached the tops of my basketball shoes. Then I took the blouse and wound it around my head like a turban.

Robbie laughed. "Wait until the TV crews get a look at you. You'll never live this down at school."

I had to admit that it was really weird to be wearing a skirt. Still, I wasn't kidding when I'd told him about the camel drivers, so if Robbie wanted to laugh, let him. I had more problems to worry about than Robbie's smirks. I bent down and picked up the hubcap tool and tried to get the hubcap off the car. I don't know what I was doing wrong, but nothing would make it come loose. I was so mad that I finally stood up and kicked the dumb thing. "Ouch!" I yelped as my foot fully felt the pain of the kick. "Darn! I guess we'll have to do without them."

"What do we need hubcaps for?"

"I was going to try to make them into a signal for any planes that might fly by. I thought the metal might reflect the sun, but nothing's gonna get the hubcaps off the car. Let's go work on making ourselves a better shady spot."

I tried to remember what else the book had said about surviving. It said something about staying cooler if you didn't sit right on the ground. You needed to be up a foot or so. I wondered if we could get one of the seats out of the car, but I didn't see how. Then I looked at the arms of the saguaro. I didn't really think they'd hold us, and besides, they were covered with cactus needles. Ouch! It hurt just to think about it. I walked back over to the car and looked again at all our stuff, wishing it would somehow turn into something great to get us out of here. Unfortunately, nothing had changed. I stared at the spare tire, and then walked over to it. I stood it on edge and began rolling it. "Hey," Robbie said, "where you going with that? You think you're going to just roll out of the desert? Get it? Roll out of the desert?"

I ignored him and rolled the tire until I could plop it down in the shady spot I'd created under the saguaros. Unfortunately, there was no way two people could fit on the tire, and no way that I knew how to get one of the other tires off the wheels. I couldn't even get the dumb hubcaps off.

The sun was making my head hurt, but I tried to think what else I could use. There was nothing big, so I started taking little rocks and even some broken cactus and piling them on top of each other. "Hey, Robbie," I called. "I could use some help here." There was no answer. It was easier to keep finding little things to pile on top of each other than to go get Robbie. Bit by bit the pile was growing higher. When it was finally as high as the tire, I headed back over to the car.

"Robbie," I yelled. "What are you doing?"

"Over here," he grunted.

I walked around the car. Robbie had gotten three hubcaps off the car and was working on the fourth. "Nice going!" I said, and I really was impressed. "Take them over to the shady spot, then come back for more stuff."

Robbie grinned. "Thanks. They weren't so easy to get off, but I did it!"

I pushed his baseball hat down on his head. Maybe we really were going to make it after all.

Eventually, we had the hubcaps and the floor mats, the gulpers, and the seat cushion. We put the gulpers in the shade, and I threw the carpeted floor mats and the seat cushion on the make-shift seats I had made. I put the hubcaps in front of us in the sun. I glanced down at my arm. My watch read 9 A.M. I couldn't believe it. How could it already feel so hot so early? All we had left to get was the Lifesavers and the cookies, and then we had to wait for what I hoped wouldn't be too long to get rescued.

As we got closer to the car, I decided we should put up the hood, so anyone from far away could see the car was in trouble. I went to the front of the car and tried to open the hood. Staring at it, I yelled to Robbie, "Hey, come here. You see any way to get this thing open?" Robbie looked, but he couldn't find any kind of handle either.

"Maybe this'll help," Robbie offered, and he banged on the hood. "Yow! My hand is burning!" he yelled, but the hood remained shut.

"Oh, never mind," I said. "Maybe the dumb thing is just broken."

Robbie looked at me. "Hey, I got another idea. Why don't we open all the doors. Then they'll have even more stuff to see."

As I was opening the car doors, I glanced inside the car, and I saw the black lever marked "hood release." I felt like an idiot. In no time, we had the hood open, and then I got another idea. I took part of the nightgown that was supposed to have been for Aunt Susan. Opening the window washer container next to the radiator, I dipped the nightgown into it. While it was still dripping with soapy water, I tore the material into strips. "Put this around the back of your neck. We can't drink the water, but we can use it to help us stay cool." I put some strips of the wet blue lacy material around my neck, and Robbie began to snicker. "If only Jennifer could see you now!"

I threw a strip around his neck. I was not going to talk about Jennifer. "Let's go sit in the shade," I said.

"Wait. Look what I thought of while you were getting the hood up." Robbie proudly pointed to the side mirrors which he had tilted upward to catch the sun's reflection. "Airplanes have to see them, don't you think?"

"Nice going, Robbie! Give me five!" I said.

Robbie looked extremely pleased with himself. "We're awesome, and we're gonna get rescued. I just know it."

We walked over to the shady area we'd made and sat down. The seats weren't the most comfortable in the world, but they weren't that awful. "So, now what?" Robbie said.

"Now, we wait." It was really hot. My shirt was already starting to stick to my skin. I tried not to think about it. When we'd moved to Arizona, I'd heard that it was hot enough during the summer to fry an egg on the sidewalk. I didn't know if that was true, but even in the city it felt like you were always sitting under a very hot heat lamp. At least there, you had air conditioning and swimming pools.

"So, how long have we been sitting here?"

I looked at my watch. "Ten minutes."

"Is that all? Are you sure your watch didn't break?"

Just then a lizard scurried past us. It ran so fast that it didn't even look like its front legs were touching the ground. "Wow, that was a humungous lizard," Robbie said. "I saw a little one outside our window the other day, but I've never seen one that big."

"Yeah. You know Gabe Morton? Well, once he went to catch one, and he said that he grabbed its tail, and the tail came off in his hand, but the lizard still kept running."

"Really?"

"That's what Gabe said." I wiped my forehead with my arm. "Tell you what, let's think about places we could be that are cool."

"Okay. How about Alaska?"

"Well, what about it?"

"I don't know. I've never been there."

I sighed. "Robbie, like this. Pretend we were in a swimming pool back in Phoenix. We jumped in the deep end, and the water was so cold that we yelled. There were goose bumps all over our skin, and we had to swim real fast to try to get warm. But even though we swam a lap, we were still shaking, and our teeth were chattering. Can you feel it? Can you see us there?"

"No, I'm still hot."

"Yeah, me too." I looked down at my watch; practically no time had passed. I wondered what they were saying about us in Phoenix. What were they doing to try to rescue us? Even the backs of my ears felt as if they were on fire.

Robbie interrupted my thoughts. "Okay, I got a cool place for us to be. We're up on the ski slopes in Flagstaff. It is so cold. It's blowing and it's snowing. We're on the chair. We get just past mid-point, and the chair stops. We sit there, and the wind and snow sting our faces. We'd give anything to get off that chair and warm up."

"That's good," I said. "You're describing last Christmas. Boy, we were freezing. I'd sure settle for a little of that icy snow right now."

Robbie nudged me. "Look quick!" He pointed, and off to our right, I saw a roadrunner zip along. It was so fast. It ran almost directly in front of us, and we both noticed that it had a firm clamp on the head of a lizard. The body was still hanging from the bird's mouth.

"Sick!" Robbie exclaimed. Then he wrinkled his forehead. "I wonder what other bugs and stuff are out here. I sure hope we don't run into our friend, the snake from last night."

I was worried about that myself, but I figured most of the animals probably slept during the day and came out at night when they didn't have to be out in the sun. I sure hoped I was right because our only weapon was a car jack, and I wasn't sure that'd be much help. I mean, suppose one of us got a poisonous bug on us; we couldn't very well hit it with the jack. I'd never seen a real scorpion, but I knew there were supposed to be scorpions in the desert. They had long curving tails filled with poison at the end, and some people died from scorpion stings. Suddenly, it felt like a spider was crawling up my leg. I jumped up and brushed myself off, but I didn't see anything.

"What's wrong?" Robbie said.

"Uhh, nothing. I just wanted to stretch. You know it's hard to keep sitting." Robbie stared at me, and then he copied Mom's I-don't-believe-you-one-bit look. He raised one eyebrow and moved his lips as if he was eating sour candy.

I wished there was something else we could do to get ourselves rescued, but I just couldn't think of anything. I crossed my fingers and hoped that wherever we were was a frequently used part of the desert. Pretty soon, Robbie got up too. He started collecting a lot of little rocks, and then he put them all down next to our "chairs."

I grabbed a handful of the rocks.

"Hey," Robbie complained. "Get your own!"

"I will," I said; "but we'll need yours too. That pile of rocks just reminded me of something I read. When you're lost you're supposed to make a big X on the ground by where you are so they can see you from the air."

In a few minutes, we had gotten enough rocks to make the X. Then we started laying the rocks out. When we were done, Robbie shook his head. "That doesn't exactly look like an X to me."

I had to agree. It was hard to see the whole X when we were so close to the ground. I stood up, took the heel of my shoe, and scraped an X into the dirt. "Now, let's fill it in with the rocks."

The sun beat down on our necks as we made it, and it felt good to sink back into our shady spot. Robbie wiped his forehead with his arm. "Boy, I sure hope they use that X to find us because it was so hot to make it!"

"I don't care what they use. I just hope they get here pretty soon."

The two of us sat under the towel. There didn't seem to be anything else to say or do, and it was really boring just sitting there. I kept looking at my watch. It seemed like we had been sitting for hours, but each time, my watch showed only a couple of minutes had passed.

Robbie started fiddling with some of the extra rocks we'd collected. "Hey," he nudged me, "let's play a game. Let's try to get the rocks into the hubcaps."

"Nah, I don't feel like it."

"Oh, come on. What else is there to do. It's boring and it's hot just to sit here."

After about fifteen minutes, we had exhausted our supply of rocks. From looking at the hubcaps, it was easy to see why Robbie was the baseball pitcher instead of me. I had no intention of collecting the rocks so that I could get beaten again, and Robbie's face was almost as red as his hair. I guess he decided it was too much work to go round them up again too.

"I wonder . . ." Robbie paused. "I wonder if I'll ever get to pitch in a baseball game again."

"Sure," I said, trying to joke. "Who ever heard of an eight-year-old's pitching arm giving out?"

"Don't treat me like such a little kid. You know what I mean! And you know I turned nine three weeks ago! I'm not staying here anymore. It's too awful just to sit here and get hotter and hotter and hotter. I'm walking out of here. We tried it your way, and nothing has happened. We haven't heard any rescue planes or helicopters. We haven't seen any Jeeps out looking for us. Face it. No one is coming. If you're too chicken to try to find your way out, you can just stay, but I'm leaving!"

"But Robbie—" He didn't listen. He stormed away from the car and the shady spot. He didn't even take any of the water with him. I didn't know what to do. There was no way he could survive if he kept walking, but it might kill us both if I tried to stop him. Tears of frustration trickled down my face. "Robbie," I yelled, "please come back here! Please, we agreed that we would stay right here. You don't know where you're going."

Robbie yelled back over his shoulder, "No, you agreed with yourself. You always want to be the one to decide." Robbie continued to walk onward. I'd have to go after him. I couldn't just let him walk to his death. I forced myself to stand up and walk out from the shady area. I took one of the gulpers and began to walk in Robbie's direction. I could probably catch Robbie. I could probably tackle him and get him to the ground. But I wasn't big enough to put him over my shoulder and make him come back. I walked a few steps. The sun seemed even stronger than it had been an hour ago. Robbie looked back over his shoulder, saw me coming, and began to run.

This was crazy! Maybe I was only making things worse by going after him. Maybe, if he didn't have to prove that I couldn't stop him from leaving, he'd just decide to come back on his own. Biting my lip, I went back to the shady spot, slammed the gulper down, and to my horror watched as the lid popped off and some of our precious water spilled out. Defeated, I sat down and stared in the direction he was going. When he looked back and saw I wasn't chasing him, he stopped running. Unfortunately, he didn't turn around, and pretty soon, he was no more than a disappearing dot. "Oh, Robbie," I called softly. "How could you do this?"

Even if by some chance I did get rescued, how could I ever live with the fact that I'd let my little brother just disappear into the desert somewhere? My throat felt like it was on fire. I reached over for the gulper and took a sip, swishing the water around my mouth to make it last longer before I swallowed it. I had to fight with myself to keep from drinking the whole gulper. Only a sip or two. I made myself cap it and put it down.

I'd hoped with everything in me that Robbie would just turn around and come back, but he hadn't. I put my hand across my eyes. I knew that I had to go out after him and try to get him water and shade. I tried hard not to let myself think that my trying to rescue Robbie would probably mean that no one would ever find either one of us.

I decided to carry the gulper with me. This time I checked it carefully to make sure that it was tightly fastened and no water would spill out of it as I carried it. Then I began to walk in the direction that I'd seen Robbie go. My skin felt like it was being burned alive. It seemed almost like I'd crawled into a giant oven, and someone had shut the door, then turned the temperature up to high. At least I was gaining on the figure in the distance. Then I realized why. It was coming toward me. I continued walking to the approaching figure. It had to be Robbie. After all, I'd seen him go off this way, and the two of us were the only ones who seemed to even know about this spot except the snakes, the coyotes, and . . . the kidnappers.

y heart was pounding as the figure came closer, and my eyes were stinging as the sweat dripped down toward them from my forehead. When it got still closer, I tried to yell, but it came out only a croak: "Robbie."

By the time he reached me, he said he felt real dizzy. "I'm sorry, you were right. Too hot. No water."

I put the gulper to his lips. He started to drink greedily, but I pulled the gulper away. "This is all the water we've got. It has to last! Come on—lean on me, and we'll go back to the shade." I put Robbie's arm around my shoulders and half-pulled, half-dragged him back to our spot. By the time we got there, I was feeling pretty dizzy myself. Robbie didn't say anything the whole way. I could hear him panting as we went. I felt so tired, I wasn't sure I could make it, but finally we got to our shaded spot. I dumped Robbie on one seat and collapsed on the other. My breathing was coming so hard that it felt like my heart was going to jump right out of my chest.

I put the gulper to my mouth and took another big swig. Then I handed it to Robbie and made him do the same. He handed the bottle back empty. The only liquid we had left was the greyish stuff from our shoes. I dipped my fingers into it and ran them around my face. Then I wetted a little piece of the blue lacy strip around Robbie's neck and wiped off his face.

"Ahhhh," Robbie screamed.

"It's water, it's just water." I shouted, my heart pounding. "Calm down."

"My arm, my arm!" Robbie grabbed at his left arm and began to rock with pain.

"What's the matter?" I screamed at him.

"I don't know. It hurts so bad!" Robbie continued to clutch his arm and moan.

I pried his fingers from his arm, and could see a big red spot that was swelling even as I watched. In the middle of the red was an almost white spot and what looked like a little puncture hole. I couldn't see a stinger, but I was pretty sure something had bitten or stung Robbie. In Boy Scouts we had learned that there were thirty-six different kinds of scorpions in Arizona, and one of them was real poisonous. *Think!* I told myself. What else did I remember about scorpions? I couldn't think of anything. Meanwhile, Robbie kept moaning, "It hurts so much."

I tried to think what I knew about any kind of bites. All I remembered was that Mom used baking soda paste if we ever got a bee sting, but that didn't help much because we didn't have any baking soda out there. Ice helped too, but we certainly didn't have any of that. I thought about something I had heard about soothing pain with aloe from the right cactus, but who knew what kind of cactus that was?

"Hey, Robbie, it's okay," I said, hoping my voice didn't sound as scared as I was. "Really, it's just a little bite or something. It'll go away."

Robbie was crying. "It was a scorpion, huh. I know it was. Did you see it? Oh, Scott, I know I got poisoned."

"Nah," I lied. "I know what a scorpion bite looks like, and this isn't one. It was probably just a dumb old ant or something. It'll stop hurting in a few minutes."

I looked at the swelling spot on Robbie's arm again. It didn't look like any ant bite I'd ever seen, but I had never seen a scorpion bite at all. I crossed my fingers and prayed that this bite was nothing. Trying to keep my voice calm, I said, "Hey, just take it easy. No point to getting all worked up over a dumb ant bite. I'm pretty sure that's all it is. Just a stupid little stinging ant. Hey, your arm'll feel better pretty soon. Just lean back," I said to Robbie. "Try to think about something else."

"Easy for you to say," Robbie muttered. "Besides, this hurts too much to be from some little old ant." Then he didn't say anything more. He just bit his lip and continued to rock back and forth holding his left arm. I wanted to say something to make it better, but I couldn't think of anything else to say, so I just patted Robbie's shoulder and hoped I was right about its being an ant.

It got real quiet. I'm not sure if we slept or not. I was feeling pretty dizzy. The sun was making everything dance in wavy lines, and I didn't know if only a few minutes or a few hours had passed when I heard Robbie say "Scott . . ." His voice was barely there. "Hey, Scott, even though we fought, I'm glad you were my brother."

Stringy cobwebs were clinging to my brain. It was hard to think, but still an alarm blared in my head. "Don't say *were,* Robbie; I *AM* your brother!"

Robbie didn't answer. It took so much effort to move, but I made myself shake his arm. "Robbie," I called, but his head had dropped down on his chest. "Not *were,* AM!" I screamed, but I don't know if it was more than a whisper. "Please, please, you can't die!"

My eyes were just slits by now, and I tried to shake my head so I could make my eyes clear and see right, but they wouldn't work. Somehow, I managed to grab for the can of gray water. Maybe if I could just cool Robbie off. I took the can and poured some water over Robbie's head. He stirred, but only a little. "Come on, Robbie, don't do this!" I forced the can to Robbie's lips and poured a little of the liquid down his throat. He gagged, and spit it out. I tried to see whether the spot on his arm was better, but my eyes wouldn't focus right.

I knew I wasn't much better off, and so I forced the little liquid left into my own parched and swollen lips. I fought waves of nausea as it went down, and then I retched.

I think the minutes crept on into hours, but my eyes were too fuzzy to see my watch. My head buzzed, and my legs felt too rubbery to ever stand up again. I was so tired. I had never been this tired in my whole life. I just wanted to sleep, but I had to do one last thing. Fumbling, I felt for the pencil and paper on the ground. When I found them, I forced my fingers to pick them up. I couldn't see well enough to read what I was writing, but I felt the pressure of my fingers moving the pencil as I wrote, "Dear Mom, We tried so hard to live. We really did love you." It was so hard to make my hand lift a stick next to me and put the paper under it, but I did it. At least, some day, if someone ever found us, Mom would get the note. I tried to lean over and hug Robbie goodbye, but my arms wouldn't move anymore. I thought I saw a snake slithering toward us, but it didn't matter. I just needed to sleep. I let my head fall to my chest, and pretty soon, I realized that I no longer felt the burning of my throat or the awful thickness of my tongue. I didn't feel hot any more. Somehow, the sun had sunk into a kind of strange darkness.

My alarm clock was buzzing. I reached out to shut it off. "Mom," I tried to say, "I still have more time to sleep; turn off my alarm!" but for some reason, my tongue seemed to take up so much of my mouth that I couldn't say the words. The buzzing sound got louder. Stupid alarm! Why wouldn't it turn off? All I wanted to do was sleep. My eyes felt like they were glued shut. I tried to push them open, but they wouldn't obey. What was wrong with my dumb body anyway! I lifted my hand to force my eye open, and my hand felt as if it weighed a million pounds. Finally, it got to my face, and pulled my unwilling eye open. Now, if I could just find my alarm clock and turn the buzzing off so I could sleep. My vision was so blurry; but wait, this didn't look any-thing like my bedroom. Where was I anyway? My whole body ached.

There were cacti . . . and then . . . then I realized where I was. The desert. Everything came rushing back to me. "Robbie," I croaked.

There was no answer from the slumped body next to me. My fuzzy brain took a minute to realize that even though my room and my alarm had been only a dream, the buzzing sound was real, and it was still going. If it wasn't my alarm clock, what was it?

I looked up in the sky. A plane. I stared into the blueness to make sure that this wasn't another dream, but there was definitely a small airplane up there circling around. An airplane that was probably looking for us! I tried to get up. If only I could just stand up and wave my arms and shout. The airplane buzzed in the sky as it flew to the south of us. I forced myself to really sit up from my slumped position. "Robbie, hang on. We're gonna be rescued." My tongue was so swollen that I didn't know if it made the actual words or not, but Robbie had to know. I pushed my hand over to him and tried to shake him. Robbie didn't answer. He almost seemed as if he were . . . I couldn't think it. It was just too awful. I wouldn't let myself think at all. I knew Robbie would be okay. I just had to hurry up and get us rescued. I put my hands on the seat I'd made and tried to push my body to a standing position, but I felt so weak. My legs were like rubber, and just as I thought I was standing up, my knees buckled and I fell. Lying on the ground, I watched the plane grow to be only a speck and heard the buzzing get further and further away. The plane hadn't seen us. Our last hope, and I hadn't been strong enough to make it see us. I began to cry, but no tears came. My throat was so parched that I sounded more like a moaning animal than a kid.

The ground was burning hot, and I knew I should drag myself back onto the seat I'd made in the shade. But it just all seemed like so much work, and pretty soon I'd be dead anyway. I lay there feeling both asleep and still vaguely awake. How could the plane have been right up there and still not have seen us! Then I heard the buzzing grow louder again. I rolled from my stomach to my back and stared into the sky as the little plane dipped down and flew almost directly overhead. "Please, please, please," I prayed. "Please see us here and help us."

No one seemed to hear those cries because the plane circled us once again and then flew away. Then I realized that something brightly colored was falling toward me. In the quiet of the desert, it smacked the ground about three feet from me. Too weak to get up and walk to it, I forced myself to crawl over the rocks to reach the bright color. Every time my already hurt knee made contact with the ground it throbbed so much that I yelped in pain, but I kept going. As I got closer, the fluorescent yellow and orange became even brighter. Finally, I sank down right next to it. I was panting like a dog and trembling all over. I forced my hand, almost clawlike, to grab what looked like a velcro black wallet with orange and yellow fluorescent stripes on it and long pink and orange fluorescent streamers attached to it. It took all my strength to tear the velcro apart. Inside was a piece of paper with bold black marker on it. If only my eyes could read it. I rubbed my eyes with the back of my hand, trying to make the words come into focus, but they were just a black blur!

Desperate, I tried moving the paper at different angles. Still, the words wouldn't come into focus. Finally, shutting one eye and squinting with the other, I read, "Help is on the way. Stay calm. Maricopa County Sheriff's Office." I grabbed the paper to my heart. I had never read more perfect words. "Help is on the way!" I repeated it again and again in my brain. We were going to be saved! "Robbie," I tried to call. "Hold on. Just hold on. We're not gonna die!"

I guess I must have blacked out again for a few minutes, because the next thing I heard was a loud noise in the sky again. I couldn't get my eyes open, but I began to feel a tremendous wind blowing, and the noise grew even louder. The next thing I knew someone was leaning over me. I grabbed his arm. "You real?" I croaked.

"I sure am," a deep voice screamed into my ear above the loud noise of the plane. "And you're going to be just fine. You just relax and let us take care of you."

"Brother," I gasped. "My brother . . ." It was so hard to make the words sound like words.

"It's okay. My partner is with your brother right now. I'm going back to the helicopter to get some water. I'll be right back."

I reached for his arm. I was afraid he'd disappear—a hallucination or my imagination. When I touched only air, I began to really wonder. Was this really help, or was I just imagining it because I wanted it so badly? Then I heard the crunch of footsteps and felt a wetness on my chest and a cool wet cloth go under my neck and around my forehead. "I'm going to give you a tiny sip of water," the deep voice said. "Swish it around in your mouth." He put something to my lips and lifted my head. I wanted to gulp gallons of water; one sip seemed almost mean.

"More," I croaked.

"Let's just see . . ." he began to say and then the sound of his voice was drowned out by another helicopter landing. Everything was blowing, and the helicopter's blades and engine were making so much noise that I couldn't hear anything. Swirling dirt and dust kept me from even thinking of opening my eyes, and then I felt myself being placed onto a gurney. A voice got right next to my ear and screamed, "We're going to lift you up now. We'll load you into the rear of the MediEvac helicopter over there, and then we'll get you to the hospital. There's a nurse on board. She'll look after you. Nod if you can hear me."

I nodded my head. I felt a strong hand grip mine for a minute, and the voice yelled into my ear again, "Son, you're a brave boy. You're going to be okay!"

I felt myself being lifted into the air, and then once I was up to the helicopter, I felt my gurney being set onto some sort of track and wheeled in. I heard it click into place. "Robbie," I tried to croak.

A woman's voice said, "They'll have him on board in a minute. Now, just let yourself relax. We're going to begin to cool you down."

I forced my eyes open. The ceiling was so close to my face. I felt new cool, wet towels being placed on me. The nurse leaned over me, checking something. "Please." I tried to make my unwilling mouth form words. "Robbie, hurt. Bitten, stung."

The nurse stopped what she was doing and took my hand. "Do you know by what?"

"No, but . . ." It was so hard to make the words form, but I had to do it. "His left arm . . . upper part."

"I can't understand you," the nurse said. "Try to say it again."

I forced my unwilling mouth and tongue to work. I thought I said it over and over, but maybe I only got the words out once before the nurse patted my arm. "That will help," she said. "Now, you relax. I'm going to start an IV."

I heard another gurney roll onto tracks in the helicopter. I felt the door slam shut, and then the noises of the helicopter drowned out everything else. I let myself lay back on the softness of the gurney and sleep. Someone else could be in charge now. "Robbie," I whispered. "We made it. We're safe! You just gotta have stayed alive."

ook, his eyes are opening," said a voice that seemed to me to be coming from far, far away.

"Uh-huh," said another, deeper voice. "He seems to be regaining consciousness."

Everything was so blurry that I couldn't see, and it hurt too much to try to keep my eyes open, so I closed them again. I wanted to ask where I was, what was happening, but though I could get my mouth open, my tongue seemed to take up my whole mouth, and I couldn't make any words work. All I knew was that I didn't feel so hot anymore. I stopped trying to think or to speak, and I just let the coolness spread over my body.

I don't know how long I stayed like that, but the next time I opened my eyes, I saw my mom's face floating right above mine. I had never realized just how pretty she was. People said that I had her blue eyes, but the way she was looking at me, hers were much better. They were so kind-looking and filled with love.

"Oh, Scott. You're going to be okay. I was so scared.

You must have been too, but you were so brave. When the Search and Rescue Team found you, they said you had done everything just right to save your lives."

My eyes began to focus. I was alive! Oh, God. I was alive! Then I remembered about the plane and the deputy and the helicopter. As the room came into view, I realized I was in a hospital. There was a tube attached to my arm. Was my little brother okay too? My swollen tongue managed to get around a word. "Robbie?" I croaked.

"The doctors say Robbie will be fine too. He's in the next bed. He had kind of a rough go of it when he first got here. But you know your brother. You can't keep him down for long." Mom smiled. "He woke up about an hour ago, pointed to his baseball cap, and when I gave it to him, he managed a grin, and then fell immediately back to sleep."

"But—the bite on his arm? Was it a scorpion? Was it poisonous?"

"Just a bee sting. I know it hurt him a lot, but Robbie isn't allergic to bees so he was okay."

I tried to smile. "We're both gonna live?"

There were tears coming down Mom's cheeks, and I felt her reach over and take my hand. "Of course, you are! Of course, you are." She wiped her tears away with her other hand. "You just rest now. After you're stronger, I'll explain everything."

As much as I wanted to know more, I couldn't keep my eyes open. I had to go back to sleep.

I don't know how long I slept, but when my eyes

flicked open the next time, I saw I was still in a hospital. It hadn't been just a wishful dream. My head was much clearer now, and my heart pounded with relief. In spite of everything, we really had made it. I turned my head and saw that Robbie was awake in the next bed. "Hey, Robbie!"

"About time you woke up!" he said, and he gave me a thumbs-up sign.

"Well, it looks as if the two of you are finally both really awake," came the booming voice of a white-coated man. He took his stethoscope and came over toward my bed. "I'm Dr. Handson."

"Have we been asleep for a long time?" I asked.

"Oh, you've both been fading in and out for awhile. Robbie gave us a scare for a little bit there, but he's a tough young man, aren't you, Robbie?"

Robbie grinned. "Yeah, I guess I am!"

The doctor examined me and then Robbie. "Well, I'd say that both of you boys certainly are doing much better. You sure had a lot of people worried about you!"

"We were pretty worried ourselves," Robbie piped in.

The doctor chuckled. "You're very popular individuals; did you know that? First, you had practically every police force in the state trying to find you, and now you have practically every newspaper, radio, and television station waiting to do an interview with you."

"We do? Wow, Scott, just like we said in the desert. Remember? Hey, how do I look?"

At that moment, Mom walked in the room with a cup of coffee. The doctor looked at her and smiled. "Your boys are both doing just fine. They'll bounce back from all this fast. A couple more days, and it will seem as if this whole thing never happened."

I didn't know about that. I didn't think I would ever forget the terrors of those days in the desert. Robbie, however, had other things on his mind. "Well, when are we gonna be on TV?"

The doctor replied, "Son, you already have been the lead story on TV and the front page of the newspaper."

A nurse came into the room. "Sorry to interrupt, but the deputies who found these boys heard that they're conscious, and want to know if they can come in."

"Oh, please, could they come in?" Mom asked the doctor. "I owe those deputies more than I could ever say."

The doctor said it would be all right, and two men in Maricopa County Sheriff's Department uniforms walked into the room holding their hats. "How are you guys doing?" asked the tallest of them.

"How'd you find us? What did you do with us? How'd you keep us alive? Were we almost dead when you found us?" Robbie began firing questions at them before I could say anything at all.

The taller deputy grinned. "Well, you are feeling better. You certainly weren't this talkative when we found you. Good thing or we'd have been too busy answering questions to rescue you!"

The other deputy turned toward Robbie. "Amazing how fast kids recuperate. These sure don't look like the two boys I put on the helicopter."

"Helicopter! We were on a helicopter? Oh, wow, and I didn't even know it. Tell me all about it!" Robbie insisted.

Looking at the two deputies, I said, "I had just about given up hope when I saw the plane in the sky, and then I didn't think the plane had seen us. It seemed to be heading away from us. Then it circled back, and it dropped that note."

"What note?" Robbie said. "I didn't see any note."

I looked at Robbie. "You were kinda out of it at the time. That was after you got stung."

"Huh," said Robbie, but instead of waiting for answers, he burst in again. "Did the plane see us because of the mirrors on the car? I was the one who put them up like that. Did you see the hubcaps? I was the one who got them off the car, but it was Scott's idea to do it."

At the rate Robbie was asking questions, we were never going to find out what happened to us. I leaned over toward him. "Robbie! Let him tell us what happened."

"I am," Robbie said. "I want to know too. So how did you find us?"

"Actually," the taller deputy said, "we had no idea where the kidnappers had taken you. We set up a hotline and had news bulletins on radio and TV asking anyone who might have seen either of you or your mom's car to call."

"Did lots of people call?" Robbie asked.

The shorter deputy with a sort of big belly answered. "We were getting reports from all across the state. One person would call and say he was sure he had seen you in the northwest corner, and then we'd get another call from someone sure that you'd just been seen crossing the border into Mexico. Though all the law enforcement agencies in the state were cooperating, we didn't get the break we needed until yesterday afternoon when we heard from a nurse in Tucson."

"Tucson?" I said, "But we weren't ever even close to Tucson."

"Right," said the taller deputy. "But the men who kidnapped you were. Yesterday, alleged drug dealers in Tucson were involved in a shootout with police. One died immediately, and the other was taken to the hospital. Right before he died, he told a nurse that he'd left a couple of kids in the desert outside of Scottsdale. She wasn't sure that she understood him or that he wasn't hallucinating. Anyway, she got called to an emergency code, and she forgot what he'd said."

Even sitting in the bed with covers, I suddenly felt myself shiver. It was just too awful to think someone knew where we were and didn't know it was important.

Robbie jumped in. "Wow, so what made her call you?"

The shorter deputy said, "Later in the day, she took a break, and while she was sitting in the nurse's lounge, someone turned on the TV. One of the news bulletins came on, and as she heard it, she suddenly thought of the dying drug dealer's words, and she began to wonder if he could have been talking about the two of you."

The deputy who'd been silent up to now broke in. "When the nurse called, she didn't sound too sure of herself, and we thought it was just one more tip to be checked out, but we followed up on it by asking a Cessna search plane to fly over the area. It was only a matter of minutes before we got a message back that they'd located the vehicle, and then they'd seen the shelter you'd made and you."

Mom had tears running down her face. "They called me right away. Those minutes until the helicopter landed and a second group of paramedics arrived were so . . ." Mom couldn't finish.

"Hey, Mom, it's okay; we're okay now," I said.

One of the deputies cleared his throat. "Well, we'll be going now, but in a few days, we'd like to talk a little with you boys about your kidnappers."

"Sure," Robbie jumped in. "I can tell you lots of stuff. One even had a tattoo, and it was a snake, and it was awful."

Before we could really thank the deputies and before they could leave, another man entered the room and introduced himself as the chief administrator of the hospital. "Dr. Handson says you boys are well enough to participate in a brief interview, and the press is all over this place." He turned to Mom. "Would it be all right for the boys to hold a very short press conference so that we could get this hospital back to normal?"

"You've all been so wonderful to us. As long as the

doctor says it's all right for the boys, we'd be glad to have the press conference."

Robbie tossed back his covers. "TV, here we come!"

"Not so fast, partner," the administrator said. "We'll have some nurses take you in wheelchairs."

"Ahh, I can walk!" Robbie exclaimed, but the doctor said Robbie might faint, and he would be taken to the press conference in a wheelchair. "No way I'm gonna faint! I've been waiting my whole life to be on TV."

We made quite a group trooping down the hall: the administrator, Mom, the deputies, and the two nurses who were pushing our wheelchairs.

"Now, there are quite a few reporters in there. I don't want it to scare you boys," warned the administrator.

"Thanks, but it would probably take quite a bit to scare us anymore," I said.

"Besides," Robbie chipped in, "we have this little bet about which one of us is going to be better on TV."

With that, the door to the temporary press room opened, and we were wheeled in. I couldn't believe the table of microphones, the cameras, and the photographers who began snapping flash photos of us. The whole room was packed. I wasn't sure what I expected, but this was unbelievable. With my eyes still trying to focus after a flash, I felt someone stick a microphone right under my nose and heard him ask me how I felt.

"I feel really glad to be alive," I said, and to my surprise, tears welled up in my eyes.

A reporter stuck a mike in front of one of the deputies.

"It's been so hot out. How do you think these boys managed to survive the dangers of the desert?"

The deputy looked right into the TV cameras. "They really used their heads. They survived because they used liquids well, created a shelter for themselves, tried to make signals, stayed with their vehicle, and never panicked."

Another reporter shouted, "How did you boys know to do all that?"

I started to open my mouth to explain, when I heard Robbie shout, "It was easy!"

"It was?" asked the reporter, and all cameras turned toward Robbie.

"Sure," he nodded and smiled. My mouth dropped open as I prepared to listen to my little brother explain how he had made all the decisions to save the day. I had to admit that he did have a flare for TV. He waited until all the reporters had gathered around him, and then he leaned forward to speak directly into the microphones. "You see, my brother, Scott, over there, he figured everything out. He learned how to drive the car, how to get more to drink, how to make shade, and how to do all the other stuff that kept us alive."

The cameras turned toward me. "That so?" called a reporter.

I couldn't believe what I'd heard Robbie say. I was in such a state of shock that he'd used his TV time to talk about me that I could hardly speak. "Well, we did work together to keep each other's spirits up," I said.

Then a reporter turned to Mom. "And how do you feel, Ma'am?"

Mom's eyes misted and her voice sounded kind of scratchy. "I feel such great joy and such appreciation to everyone who reached out to help my sons. I'm so proud of the way they handled themselves, and believe me— I'll never leave the keys in the car again, not even for a second." Mom leaned over and hugged Robbie and me.

Finally, the press conference was over. We were back in our hospital beds, and I had to admit that I was feeling much more tired than I'd thought I would. Dr. Handson looked at Mom and ordered her to go downstairs and get something to eat. "Oh, I really don't want to leave the boys. I can just get another cup of coffee at the nurses' station."

Dr. Handson remained firm. "The boys are fine now. You are going to get some nourishment for yourself besides coffee. They'll be well looked after by the nurse." He winked at her. "Listen, I have a feeling it will take all your strength to keep up with the mischief these two create, so you'd better take care of yourself."

Mom smiled, and I wondered if she was thinking about the hose we'd brought in the house or some of our other stunts this summer. "They certainly can create their fair share of mischief, that's for sure." Then her eyes filled with tears. "I'm just so glad they're back. . . . For a while, I almost thought . . ." Dr. Handson went over and patted her shoulder. "The boys are fine, I promise. Now, downstairs with you for some food; the nurse and I will monitor the boys." Mom blew us a kiss, and she said she'd be right back. The doctor and nurse checked us over again, and then they left the room with strict instructions that we were to stay put. I turned to Robbie, and yawning, I said, "Pretty amazing, huh?"

Robbie leaned over on his side. "I'd say. Do you realize that in three days' time we got kidnapped, almost shot, left in the desert, drove a car, almost died, rode a helicopter, and we just had as big a press conference as the President of the United States."

It was all pretty unbelievable, and in its way so was something else. "Hey, Robbie, I . . . uh . . . I just want to say thanks for the stuff you said in the desert and the stuff you said on TV about my saving us. That was really something."

Robbie looked worried. "Yeah, well, that doesn't mean I'm gonna say nice stuff about you all the time. Because I can't. I don't even want to try!"

I smiled, "No problem." And just before I drifted off to sleep, I whispered, "You just wait until you see who really looks the best on TV."

"Oh, it'll for sure be me!" Robbie declared, and then he grinned. "But we can fight about it for the whole rest of the summer!"

ABOUT THE AUTHOR

An award-winning writer and teacher, Terri Fields has lived in Arizona for the past twenty-nine years. She has been named to the All USA First Teacher Team of twenty-three of the nation's most oustanding teachers. Fields is also the author of fourteen published books and is currently working on her latest survival adventure novel, *Missing in the Mountains*.

On her office wall, she keeps a map with pins in it showing all the states and countries from which kids have written to her about her books.

Terri and her husband, Rick, have two children, Lori and Jeff.

A preview of
another exciting title from

rising moon

Books for Young Readers from Northland Publishing

QUEST
for the EAGLE
FEATHER

by
JOHN DUNCKLEE

After their evening meal, the boys hung the deer carcass high up in an aspen sapling to keep it away from cougars and bears. That night as Quiet Water kept watch, he heard a cougar growl nearby. He turned toward the sound, and tossed more wood on the fire.

Suddenly he saw the firelight bounce off two yellow eyes. The cougar stood near the tree from which the carcass hung. It growled slowly. Without taking his eyes away from the cougar's, Quiet Water stepped over to where his companions slept and shook their feet. "Wake up," he whispered. "Cougar."

Running Fox and Screaming Crow woke quickly and followed Quiet Water to the fire. The cougar was still nearby, watching them, its yellow eyes reflecting in the firelight. "If we throw a burning log toward the cougar, maybe it'll be frightened and leave us alone," Screaming Crow said.

"It smells the deer carcass," Running Fox said. "It won't be frightened for long."

"I would rather give the deer to the cougar than ask for a fight," Quiet Water said. "It's too dark to take a chance with our arrows."

"I think the best we can do is try to scare it away," Running Fox said. "I'll bet a flaming branch will make him think twice about coming any closer to our camp."

"Until he remembers the fresh meat again," Screaming Crow said.

The yellow eyes disappeared. The cougar growled again, and then they heard the large lion leaping at the deer carcass.

Running Fox reached for a burning branch from the fire and threw it toward the tree. The big cat yowled and crashed through the aspen grove to escape from the firebrand.

Screaming Crow tended the fire while the other two tried to sleep. The cougar's low growl in the distance made him keep the fire burning brightly. He had an arrow ready in his bow in case the cougar decided to return.

Running Fox kept his vigil the same way. The cougar's slow and guttural growl persisted until the first morning light.

Before waking the others, Running Fox walked to the aspen sapling that held the deer. Claw marks gouged the bark below the hanging carcass. Running Fox lowered it and sliced off enough meat for their morning meal, then hoisted it out of the cat's reach again. He laid the meat on the coals and woke his friends.

After finishing the tasty venison, they prepared for the morning's climb. Running Fox suggested they take a short cut he had noticed. "It is a steeper climb," he said. "But the distance is shorter if we go by way of the rock overhang."

Quiet Water and Screaming Crow voiced no objection to the idea. They gathered their bows and arrows and started toward the steep slope leading to the peak of the Sacred Mountain. The loose rocks along the route made the climb difficult. Their progress toward the summit slowed. "Once we pass the rock overhang, the footing should be better," Running Fox said.

"That's if we ever reach the overhang without sliding back down to the meadow," Screaming Crow said.

"We'll be bare-footed by the time we reach the top," Quiet

Water said. "These rocks are sharp, and we will probably spend all day tomorrow patching our moccasins."

They had nearly reached the rock overhang when a female cougar came out of a dark entrance, inspected the intruders, and growled fiercely. The three climbers stopped short, and looked at their challenger, all quickly notching arrows on their bowstrings. "It's a female," Screaming Crow whispered. "By the look of her belly, she's nursing cubs."

"She is probably our visitor from last night," Quiet Water said. He touched the special arrow in its quiver.

"If she turns toward us," Running Fox said, "I can put an arrow through her heart."

"She will stay where she is unless we go closer," Screaming Crow said. "We should go back, and climb the ridge again. I don't want to take a chance on making her come for us. She's big and fast and she'll be hard to stop with our arrows. She will defend her cubs, and we could end up being her food."

"If we go back down we might miss watching the eagle fly," Running Fox said.

"The eagle will fly when the eagle wants to fly," Quiet Water said. "The sooner we leave the mother cougar alone with her cubs, the better."

Quiet Water had been following his friends along the trail. He turned and began the descent over the loose rocks. The other two backed down as the female cougar stood her ground, sounding her guttural growl in front of her den.

OTHER BOOKS FROM NORTHLAND PUBLISHING: